Readers love

Connie Bailey

I0667158

Kaji Sukoshi & The Shining One

"I recommend this story to anyone who believes in true love and that wishes can come true if you are willing to fight for them." —Rainbow Reviews

"…subtle, touching, sweet and understated." —Fallen Angel Reviews

Miles to Go

"I loved this book from start to finish and couldn't put it down."

—Rainbow Reviews

A great story! —Joyfully Reviewed

Revenant

"…a tale that is thrilling and tragic and truly unique." —Book Wenches

"If you are looking for a story that has a bit of sex mixed with gothic horror then *Revenant* is a story you are sure to enjoy." —Fallen Angel Reviews

True Blue

"An excellent book not to be missed." —Literary Nymphs

"Connie Bailey sucks you in from the opening line…" —Fallen Angel Reviews Recommended Read

NOVELS BY CONNIE BAILEY

Kaji Sukoshi & The Shining One
Miles to Go
Revenant
True Blue

Something
for *Nothing*

Connie Bailey

Dreamspinner Press

Published by
Dreamspinner Press
4760 Preston Road
Suite 244-149
Frisco, TX 75034
http://www.dreamspinnerpress.com/

Something for Nothing

Cover Art by Anne Cain   annecain.art@gmail.com
Cover Design by Mara McKennen

ISBN: 978-1-61581-526-5

Printed in the United States of America
First Edition
June, 2010

eBook edition available
eBook ISBN: 978-1-61581-527-2

For one magnificent lady
and five phenomenal guys
who make this world a better place.

chapter **One**

THE noise rose above the usual feeding-time-at-the-zoo level and Martin Cruz looked up from his desk with a glare that had no perceivable effect. He folded the note he'd just finished writing and sourly regarded the nineteen behavioral problems he sarcastically referred to as students. Not one was doing anything remotely resembling learning. When he'd come here in 1988 with his degree in sociology, he'd thought he'd make a difference in the lives of some misunderstood kids, the kids none of the other schools would take. After twelve years, he'd come to realize that he was the only one here who cared about education; *Nuestra Senora Providencia Escuela para Niños*—Our Lady of Providence School for Boys—in Los Angeles wasn't much more than a warehouse for misfits, drones, and the underprivileged. Nowadays, he came to work on time, kept his head down for eight hours, and went home at the end of the day to a house whose payments he could barely afford in a neighborhood that was relatively quiet. He called roll, handed out assignments, and gave tests in the sure knowledge that none of it mattered. Except for the handful of problem children from wealthy homes, not one of these boys was going anywhere but out onto the streets and into a dead end job. Junior gangsters and future minimum wage slaves every one of them.

Mr. Cruz sighed and tried to choose one of them to do an errand. His gaze skipped over the quartet with close-cropped hair, visible piercings, and school uniform trousers tucked into combat boots. He likewise ignored the three with the makeup and rainbow hair colors as well as the skater boy contingent with their ubiquitous skull motif. On the verge of choosing from the largest group, the ones he thought of as the sheep, his eye fell on the still figure of Alvaro Torres at the back of the room.

As always, Alvaro was flanked by Enrique "Kiki" Viera and Leo Lazaro, the school's odd couple. Mr. Cruz didn't think of the trio as a gang, more like a pack. They didn't start trouble simply to relieve their boredom or because they'd fabricated a rivalry with another group, but if they felt attacked, their response was fierce and united. The teacher's gaze lingered with disapproval on their clothing. Though each wore the standard white Oxford shirt, Kiki had added ostentatious cuff links and an ascot with a stickpin. The sleeves of Leo's gray jacket were pushed up to reveal bare forearms with tribal tattoos. Alvaro's shirt was untucked and his jacket hung over the back of his chair. Instead of the required black gabardine trousers, all three were wearing blue jeans festooned with chains hanging from the belt loops. For some reason, the personal touches they added to their uniforms bothered Mr. Cruz more than the all-out costumes of the skinheads, the Goths, and the others he labeled *conforming non-conformists*. Alvaro's friends were true individuals, unconcerned with what anyone else thought of their taste, and that —in Mr. Cruz's estimation—was much more dangerous than an army of leather-clad self-proclaimed rebels. The teacher sighed again; at least Alvaro's posse wasn't the usual loud, attention-seeking type that roamed the campus. In fact, they shunned contact with anyone outside their circle. In a prime example of how life loved irony, their wish to be left alone made them more rather than less attractive. They couldn't rightly be called popular, but they were certainly the most imitated, which translated—in high school as in the rest of life—as *cool*.

"Alvaro!" Mr. Cruz pitched his voice to cut through the racket.

Alvaro didn't look up from the ink pen tattoo that Kiki was drawing on the inside of his wrist. Kiki paused as he glanced away from his work, his eyes flicking from Alvaro's downcast gaze to Leo. Leo met Kiki's eyes briefly, just long enough to affirm solidarity before he looked back down at the half-finished Mayan design like the ones he sported.

"Alvaro Torres!" Mr. Cruz repeated, almost shouting. "I need you to take a message to the main office."

"What will you give me?" Alvaro responded.

"What will I give you?" Mr. Cruz repeated incredulously.

"I can't do something for nothing," Alvaro said as Leo and Kiki smirked. "You have to make it worth my while."

The teacher had expected anything from sullen compliance to sullen refusal, but asking for payment was a new tack, and it threw him off balance. Before he could form a reply, the door opened and a young man in a mismatched uniform slouched in. Stopping in front of Mr. Cruz's desk, the newcomer stood with his head down and waited. "Well, who are you?" Mr. Cruz asked, irritated that the student hadn't knocked. The new boy's reply was nearly inaudible as he handed Mr. Cruz a piece of paper. The teacher looked at the transfer form and verified that he had a new student. "Candelario Carlisle," Mr. Cruz said. "That's not a name we see often, and it's very irregular, transferring so near the end of the year."

The boy shrugged.

"Do you prefer being called Cande, or by your full name?"

The new kid shrugged again, and Mr. Cruz made a note in his grade book.

"Whoa!" Kiki said under his breath as Candelario Carlisle half-turned toward the classroom. "The new kid's really pretty!"

Alvaro glanced up as if he hadn't been stealing looks at the new kid since the door had opened. Even under the wan fluorescent lighting, Cande's golden brown hair had a rich reddish gloss that drew the eye. His finely carved features were shadowed by thick bangs that made it impossible to determine the color of his eyes, but his most prominent feature was a pair of perfect lips that looked permanently poised for a kiss. "He's pretty," Alvaro said with a shrug and made a joke. "If you like that type."

Leo grinned and tousled Kiki's loose, dark curls. "Is the new kid your type?" he teased.

Kiki flicked Leo's hand away and straightened his subtly patterned silk scarf. "What business is it of yours?" he inquired. "Unless you're looking for a date."

Alvaro looked down to hide his smile, and when he looked up again, he caught Cande looking at him. Their eyes met, and for a space of time that couldn't be quantified by things like clocks or reality, they were like two people who've grabbed hold of the same high voltage wire. Mr. Cruz said Cande's name and the spell was broken; Alvaro turned quickly away, facing backward in his chair.

"I reserve the desks in the two front rows for proven troublemakers," Mr. Cruz said. "There's an empty chair in the back left corner. You can sit there for now."

Cande didn't respond by as much as a nod. He plodded to the back of the room and set his backpack on the desk. Taking out a notebook, he sat and started doodling on a page marked by music staffs. In moments, he was in his own world, blocking out the chaos around him.

"Well, I guess our company isn't good enough for the princess," Kiki said wryly.

"He's wearing a public school jacket that's too small and…." Leo looked to Kiki. "What school wears navy trousers?"

"How would I know?"

"You're the fashion expert."

"School uniforms aren't fashion." Kiki looked over at Alvaro, expecting him to chime in, but Alvaro was watching Cande from the corners of his eyes. Smacking Alvaro's shoulder, Kiki got his attention. "What's the fascination?"

"What?"

"You're staring at the new kid."

"No I'm not."

"Not now you're not, but you were."

"That's crap." Alvaro glanced up at the clock and pulled his jacket on in anticipation of the lunch bell. "Anyone got extra money today?"

"Don't worry about it," Kiki said. "I've got you covered."

Alvaro nodded his thanks. "I'll pay you back on Monday."

"Didn't I just say not to worry about it?" Kiki looked up at Leo. "Can I buy you lunch, too, you sexy thing?"

"As long as you don't expect me to put out," Leo answered.

"Woo!" Kiki grinned and held up his hand for a high-five. "Leo shoots and scores!"

"He scored on you," Alvaro pointed out.

Kiki shrugged. "I appreciate a good return, even if it's aimed at me."

The bell rang and nineteen young men jumped to their feet with the clatter of chair legs on a wooden floor and an upsurge of conversation. Alvaro threw an arm around Kiki's neck and pulled him in close. "I love your sense of humor," he said.

"What about me?" Leo asked as he fell into step with his friends.

"You want some of this?" Alvaro put his other arm around Leo. "Come on, bitches," he said, taking the hallway that led to the cafeteria. "Let's roll."

Cande didn't rise from his seat until the room was empty except for Mr. Cruz. Under the teacher's impatient eye, he fastened the buckle on his backpack and trudged out the door.

"I HAVE to leave early today," Alvaro said as he balled up his cardboard food tray. Barely turning his head, he tossed the piece of trash into a bin about fifteen feet away.

Kiki nodded. "I'll get your geography homework and drop it by on my way home." He stretched out his legs on the grass and leaned back on his hands, turning his face to the sky. "I wish we could have class outside."

Leo nodded vehement agreement. "On the baseball field would be good."

Kiki smiled. "You're such a jock," he said as Alvaro got to his feet.

"See you later, Kiki," Alvaro said. "And Leo, don't forget to put your jacket back on before you go to class. If you get in trouble one more time, you'll get expelled."

"It's a nice look for him though, don't you think?" Kiki asked, plucking at the fringe where Leo had ripped the sleeves from his button-down shirt.

"Looking good; shows off your muscles," Alvaro said. "Just don't forget your jacket." Flashing his friends a peace sign, he walked away.

"HEY, *maricon*, give me a cigarette." Chuy Alvarez stopped in front of Kiki, his shadow falling over the other young man.

"It's the year 2000; nobody smokes anymore," Kiki said as Leo got to his feet. "Haven't you heard, *cabron*? Cigarettes are for losers,"

"Are you calling me a loser?" Chuy's pride was as prickly as his spiked crewcut.

"Why don't you go try your tough guy act on someone else, punk?" Leo said, bumping chests with Chuy. "No one here is impressed."

Chuy's pals took a step forward, but Leo's eyes stayed locked on Chuy. The punk saw nothing in Leo's unwavering gaze that said Leo would back down an inch. "If you don't have cigarettes, give me some money to buy some," Chuy said. "You're rich, Viera. Give us some money."

"My parents are rich," Kiki said. "But they don't like me. If they did, why would they send me here?"

"Ha ha." Chuy shoved at Leo, stepping back at the same time. "You fairies aren't worth the time it would take to kick your asses."

"You sound like busy guys," Kiki said, accepting Leo's offer of a hand as he stood up. "You probably have somewhere else you need to be."

"Come on." Chuy gestured to his gang. "Let's ditch these *losers* and go find somebody with money."

Kiki rolled his eyes as the four young men swaggered off. "Who are they kidding?"

"None of them would last five minutes on the street," Leo said. "I hate those little Nazi wannabes."

"Really? I couldn't tell by the way you were looking at Chuy." Kiki chuckled as they headed for the main building. They were starting up the steps when he laughed again. "Seriously, I know you're badass, but you've really gotten good at *looking* badass. I thought Chuy was going to piss his pants when you stood up to him."

Leo shrugged off the praise. "Speaking of pants pissing...." He focused on something over Kiki's right shoulder. "What do you want? I don't have time to change your diaper."

Kiki turned, knowing he'd see Eligio Domingo. The second-year student idolized Alvaro and—by extension—Alvaro's friends. "Why are you pestering us in public?" Kiki asked. "You know the rules."

"We can't be seen with you," Leo clarified, making a shooing gesture at beanpole Eligio. "Run along, nerd, before a strong wind comes and blows you away." Leo puffed out his cheeks.

"I'm looking for Alvaro," Eligio said.

"I never would have guessed," Kiki said. "Alvaro had to leave early today. You missed him by about five minutes. Hey!" Kiki frowned as Eligio took off running. "What's up his butt?" he wondered aloud.

"Kids are jumpy these days. Not like when I first came here."

Kiki chuckled. "Tell me about the olden days, grandfather," he said as they walked toward their next class.

"ALVARO!" Eligio yelled. "Alvaro, wait!"

Alvaro stopped jogging at the edge of the school parking lot and looked back to see Eligio on a rattletrap bicycle. "Where'd you get that piece of shit?"

Eligio ignored the question. "You have to come with me," he panted.

"No I don't. I have to go home."

"Please. Someone needs help."

"Kiki!" Alvaro said under his breath as he started back down the street.

"No, not Kiki. It's the new kid. Chuy's bullying him."

Alvaro stopped. "Why are you bothering me with this? All Chuy wants is his lunch money."

"That's how it started," Eligio said. "But the new kid wouldn't give him anything."

"Then he'll take a couple of punches. Big deal."

"Alvaro, please. They're really going to hurt him."

"*Chingada*! I don't have time for this."

Eligio looked at the ground. "Remember last year when Chuy was bothering me every day? Remember what I told you? What he tried to make me do?"

"Of course. I kicked his ass behind the arcade the next Saturday."

"He's trying the same thing with the new kid."

"*Aiy*," Alvaro groaned again. "Give me your bike."

"Climb on behind," Eligio said.

Alvaro put his feet on the extended rear axle, grabbed onto Eligio's shoulders, and Eligio put his long legs to work pedaling them over to the gymnasium. As they rounded the corner of the big building, they saw a group of young men near the air-conditioning unit.

Motioning to Eligio to take off, Alvaro moved stealthily along the wall until he was within earshot.

"Are you ready to give me what I want?" Chuy asked his latest victim.

Two of Chuy's gang held Cande with his arms twisted behind his back. Cande's delicate features were tense with strain, but none of the pain he was feeling showed in his soft voice when he answered. "No, I need another minute to think about it."

Alvaro suppressed a smile; he appreciated Cande's attitude, but this was about to get even uglier. The new kid already had a split lower lip, and the fourth member of Chuy's group was pawing through his backpack. If the punks didn't find anything they considered worthwhile, they were apt to give Cande a real beating for smarting off to them. New students didn't have friends yet, and jerks like Chuy felt safe messing with them. Normally, Chuy would be right, but today Alvaro didn't feel like minding his own business. He was about to step away from the concealment of the vertical duct when Chuy started talking again.

"You seriously don't want to fuck around with me."

"You said that already," Cande told him.

"He isn't hiding any money in here," said the thug rifling the backpack. "Just books and junk."

"So you don't have any smokes and you don't have any food and you don't have any money," Chuy said grabbing the front of Cande's shirt. "What good are you?"

"I don't know."

"You look like a girl."

"You said that already too."

"Did I say blow me?"

"Not in so many words, but I figured you'd get around to it eventually, you big closet case."

"What?" Chuy looked confused, which was not necessarily a good thing. When he didn't know what to do, he fell back on violence. "Are you calling me queer?"

"It sounded like you asked me to blow you. That's kind of queer, isn't it?"

Alvaro bit back a chuckle. The new kid was practically begging for an ass-kicking, but he was doing it with style, a quality Alvaro appreciated. Style was free to some, and others couldn't buy it for any amount of money. Being stylish was something Alvaro could do as well as the richest kid in school, and that was important to him.

"You're about to be very sorry," Chuy told Cande. "First, I'm going to kick your ass, and then you're going to blow me." He pulled back his fist, and his friends tightened their grip on Cande's arms. Alvaro got ready to intervene when one of the gang pulled a piece of cloth from the backpack, and the new boy began to thrash like a landed trout.

"Put it back!" Cande shouted, twisting and flailing. His elbow connected with the ribs of one of the boys holding him, and the punk let go with a cry of pain. Lunging toward the one holding the cloth, Cande nearly wrenched his other captor's arm out of the socket. Chuy moved to block him, and Alvaro came out of hiding.

"Not so fast," he said, stepping into Chuy's path. "Let the boy go and let's see what happens."

"Are you crazy?" Chuy said. "It's still four against two."

"Yeah, but we both know you're a coward," Alvaro said. "Call your assholes off and give Carlisle his backpack."

"Sounds like you want me to give you something for nothing," Chuy sneered.

Cande swung at one of the punks as another slammed into his back. As he turned to throw a punch with his left, someone grabbed his other arm. Alvaro shook his head, gesturing at the uneven fight with one hand to draw Chuy's attention as he hit him in the side with the other. As the gang leader doubled over, breathless from the sucker punch, Alvaro took three long strides and kicked the guy restraining

Cande's right arm. The thug went to the ground, rolling around as he clutched his knee. One of the other two turned to face Alvaro. Alvaro ducked a punch and head-butted the other young man in the stomach. The punk reeled back and collided with his friend, bouncing off into Alvaro's roundhouse kick. Cande caught the other one on the rebound and slung him away in the direction of the wall. Scooping up his backpack, Cande started to take off.

"Hey, new kid!" Alvaro called out as Chuy and his bullies regrouped. "It's not over."

"Damn right it isn't," Chuy said. "I think you broke one of my ribs."

"Hey!" Alvaro called to Cande again. "Come back! We're not out of trouble yet."

"You are now," Leo said as he arrived with Kiki and Eligio. "Step aside and let me take care of your light work for you."

Alvaro looked at Chuy. "It looks like there are five of us and four of you. Is it over now?"

"Yo, Chuy Alvarez," Kiki said. "You can count, right?"

"He can count," Leo said as Chuy and his gang slunk away with muttered threats and rude gestures. "What a bunch of punks."

Kiki put a hand on Alvaro's shoulder and looked into his face. "Are you okay?"

"I'm fine. Lost a little skin on my knuckles. Hey, Carlisle, are you all right?"

Cande looked up from stuffing the piece of cloth in his backpack. He nodded as he hefted the bag to his shoulder and started to shuffle off.

"Hang on," Alvaro said. "Come here for a minute. Look at you. You're a mess."

"A bloody mess," Kiki elaborated. "You should go to the school nurse."

"I can't get in trouble on my first day," Cande said. "I'll wash up in the bathroom."

Alvaro shook his head. "That won't be good enough. You need more than soap and water. You'd better come home with me." He turned to Kiki. "I really have to run. See you around four." After taking a few steps, he looked at Cande over his shoulder. "Let's go," he said in a tone that brooked no arguments.

Cande followed Alvaro, keeping pace as the tall boy steadily increased his speed to a run. When they stopped at a storefront grocery, Alvaro looked at Cande with a little more respect. "You're in decent shape," he said as he opened a gate onto an alley between the shops. "Do you play a sport?"

Cande shook his head as he followed Alvaro up a flight of stairs on the outside of the building.

"No? I'm into kickboxing right now." Alvaro demonstrated one of the martial art's circular kicks as they reached the second story landing. When Cande dodged back against the railing, Alvaro grabbed his forearm and pulled him back. "That wood's rotten," he said, loosening his grip, his fingers sliding down to curl around Cande's wrist. Cande pulled his hand free and stuck it in his pocket. After a few seconds of awkward silence, Alvaro opened the door, and they entered a tiny apartment.

"It's me, Mama," Alvaro called out before steering Cande into a miniature kitchen. "Make some tea," he said. "You know how to make tea, right? I'll be back in a few minutes."

Cande found everything he needed among the sparse supplies, boiled some water, and added the tea. When Alvaro hadn't returned by the time the tea had steeped, Cande ventured into the narrow hall. Through an open door at the end, he saw a woman sitting up in bed with her long hair loose on her shoulders. As he watched, Alvaro leaned forward into his field of vision and took the woman's hand. She continued to stare straight ahead, and Alvaro stood up. Cande spun around and tripped over his own feet. By the time he recovered and hurried into the kitchen, he knew Alvaro had seen him. "I'm sorry," he said, when Alvaro joined him. "I didn't mean to spy."

"Don't worry about it."

"I hope I didn't disturb your mother."

"She didn't even know you were there."

"Is she sick?"

"Sort of. Basically, she just stopped caring about anything after my dad left."

"Oh." Cande looked away from Alvaro. "The tea's ready."

"Yeah, smells good. Why don't you have a cup while I take some to Mama, and then I'll get you cleaned up?" Alvaro carried a cup into the bedroom and came back a few minutes later. "Come on," he said and led the way to a small bathroom. "Have a seat on the toilet." Cande sat down while Alvaro set out a few things. The sharp smell of alcohol permeated the air as Alvaro swabbed the dried blood from Cande's face. Alvaro knew the alcohol stung like fire, but Cande sat without flinching until the clean up was done. "Good man," he said absently as he began to inspect the damage. "You've got a split on your lower lip and one over your left eye. The nosebleed has stopped, and I don't think your nose is broken. You're going to have some impressive bruises, though." Alvaro turned Cande's head toward the light again. "I can put a couple of stitches in the cut on your brow bone, if you want."

"No thanks!" Cande tried to stand, but Alvaro stopped him with a hand on his shoulder.

"Okay, no stitches, but I need to put some antibiotic salve on the cuts and some butterfly closures at least."

"You have those?"

"Mama was a nurse before she lost interest in everything."

"I'm sorry."

"Thanks, but it's got nothing to do with you."

"Okay." Cande looked down at his hands as Alvaro deftly applied a couple of small butterfly bandages to the cut over his eye. "Thanks for keeping those guys from, you know, doing freaky things to me."

"Freaky things?"

"Well, you know, sexual things. I can take a beating but… anyway, thanks."

"You might want to reserve your thanks if you think gays are freaks."

"What?"

"I might be gay for all you know."

"That's not what I meant," Cande said. "I don't care if you're gay. I just don't want to be forced to do anything."

"I didn't say I was gay." Alvaro paused. "And I understand about not wanting to be forced into something."

After several seconds of silence, Cande mumbled, "I sort of like guys."

"What? Why would you tell me something like that when you don't know me?"

"You brought it up when you said you might be gay for all I knew. I thought you were hinting around. I'll shut up now."

Alvaro smiled. "What are you really saying? You're gay if I am?"

Cande's gaze brushed Alvaro's before dropping to his hands again. "Something like that. Can we talk about something else now?"

"Sure." Gently, Alvaro touched Cande's bottom lip. "Does it hurt much?"

"It hurts a lot."

"It'll hurt worse tomorrow and you'll look terrible."

Cande sighed. "My first day and I've already been in a fight and skipped my last two classes."

"A real *delicuendo*." Alvaro grinned. "Come on back in the kitchen and I'll heat something up."

"Didn't you just have lunch?" Cande asked as he followed.

"Yeah, but kicking ass on punks like Chuy Alvarez gives me an appetite. If you're not hungry, you can watch me eat… unless you have to get home."

Cande shook his head. "No one's expecting me." He looked into the pot Alvaro was putting on the two burner stove. "Just rice and beans?"

"What's wrong with that?"

"Nothing… if you don't care what it tastes like."

"I've got seasonings in there, but if you think you can do better…." Alvaro stepped away from the stove.

"Of course I can," Cande said, already reaching for items he'd noticed earlier. "Can you be somewhere else? It's a little cramped for two people."

Thrown out of his own kitchen, Alvaro gave Cande an odd look behind his back. "Sure. No problem. I'll check on Mama and get in a little practice. How long do I have?"

"It'll be ready when it's ready," Cande said, his attention on the chopping board.

"That's helpful," Alvaro snorted. When he realized he wasn't going to get an answer from the absorbed cook, he went down the hall. After turning on the television and putting the remote near his mother's hand, he went up to the roof to practice kickboxing. As always, the martial art forms began to flow into dance steps that covered every foot of the available space. As he leaped over an air-shaft cap and did a one-handed cartwheel, he saw Cande watching him from the top of the fire stairs.

"Is the food ready?" Alvaro asked. Cande nodded and turned away. Alvaro hurried after him, sniffing appreciatively as they entered the apartment. "Wow. That really smells good. I'll just change my shirt and be right back." Alvaro walked down the hall, pulling his T-shirt over his head. Cande watched the play of hard muscles under smooth brown skin before he spun abruptly and went to the stove.

When Alvaro returned to the kitchen, Cande handed him a large bowl. Alvaro lifted the dish to his face and breathed in the fragrant steam. "This smells amazing," he said as he scooped a bite from the bowl with his fingers. "It tastes even better than it smells."

"It'll taste even better from a fork. You have terrible manners."

"*Lo siento.*" Alvaro grinned as he set his bowl on the counter. "I also apologize for the lack of a table. Me and Mama usually eat in her room while she watches TV."

"I don't mind eating standing up."

Alvaro took another bite, and his eyes rolled back. "This is really, really good. What did you put in it?"

"None of your business." Cande hid a small smile behind his spoon. "But surely you can taste the chilies."

"I wondered why my tongue was on fire. How many peppers did you use?"

"You need to buy more," Cande answered around a mouthful.

Alvaro chuckled as he reached over the other boy's head for an empty bowl. He filled it halfway and carried it into his mother's room. In a few minutes, he returned with an unreadable expression. "She said it's good."

"Thank her for me."

"You don't get it. She goes for days without speaking and when she talks, it's usually to the people on television. For her to comment on food...." Alvaro caught Cande's eyes and held them. "That's a big deal around here."

Cande looked away from the sparkle of extra moisture in Alvaro's eyes. "I'm glad she likes it," he said softly.

"If I paid you would you come over once a week and make a big pot of something?"

"You wouldn't have to pay me. Just buy what I need to make the food."

"I have to pay you one way or another. Nobody does something for nothing."

"Then consider it my thanks for rescuing me." Cande picked up his backpack. "I should probably go now."

"Oh... okay." Alvaro stood aside so the other boy could pass by. "Hey, I hope I didn't make you feel funny by offering you money."

"No. That didn't make me feel funny." Cande had a vivid mental image of Alvaro moving fluidly to unheard music, of his bare back as he moved down the hallway. "Thank you… for everything."

"We're even." Alvaro watched Cande walk to the front door, surprised by how disappointed he was that the new kid was leaving. "I'll see you at school tomorrow."

"Sure," Cande said as he opened the door.

"Hey, can I ask you one thing before you go?"

"What is it?"

"What's with the last name?"

Cande's face went still, devoid of all expression. "Why?"

"You don't look like anybody else I know so I was just wondering."

"My dad was a white guy that took off before I was born. I never met him. My mother gave me up for adoption right after she squeezed me out."

"Oh. You don't have to talk about it if you don't want to."

"Cool." Cande nodded and slipped through the door, closing it gently behind him. Alvaro saw Cande's sculpted profile limned against the sun, his red-gold hair making a spiky halo, and then he descended out of sight. Alvaro went back to the kitchen, finished his food, and ate another half bowl. He fetched his mother's empty bowl and put it in the sink. Halfway through the washing up, someone knocked on the door. Recognizing the pattern, Alvaro yelled for Kiki to come in.

"What's that awesome smell?" Kiki asked as he dropped his book bag on the counter. In another moment, he was leaning on Alvaro's shoulder trying to see into the pot on the stove.

"Want some?" Alvaro asked with a trace of reluctance.

"I'm starving," Kiki said already reaching for the ladle. "Got a tortilla?" Alvaro handed him one and watched as he filled and rolled it. "How's your mama?" Kiki asked as he took a bite of the pillow-sized burrito.

"Same as always." Alvaro slung the damp dishtowel over his shoulder and dipped the ladle in the pot. He took a bite from the serving spoon, ignoring Kiki's grimace at his bad manners. "Cande Carlisle made this."

"Really? The new kid has hidden talent." Kiki took another big bite. "This is really good."

"I can't believe he made it with nothing but what we had in the kitchen. My cooking never tastes like that."

Kiki eyed his burrito filling. "Looks like rice, beans, and a lot of peppers. Plus some other stuff. I don't know." He shrugged. "It tastes good."

"What's my homework like?"

"I already did it. I don't want you wasting your time on geography when you have better things to do."

"Like practicing for the festival?"

"You know it!" Kiki finished his food in two gigantic bites. "Come on. Let's go. Leo's dinner break starts in ten minutes."

Alvaro called goodbye to his mother, and he and Kiki walked the eight blocks to the garage where Leo worked after school. They met Leo out back where the mechanics went to smoke when the weather was good. After they moved the picnic table, they had a twenty by twenty slab of concrete to practice on. They warmed up with a few stretches, and Leo turned on the boom box. Two men in coveralls watched and made joking comments as Alvaro, Leo, and Kiki worked on their dance routine until Leo's dinner hour was almost up. Alvaro and Kiki hung out while Leo hurriedly ate the burrito Alvaro had brought.

"Man, I can't wait until I can quit this job," Leo said as he got back into his coveralls. "I need something that pays better."

"When you're a star, you can have your own mechanic," Kiki said.

"Yeah? Well, I'll treat him a lot better than these jerks treat me."

Alvaro patted Leo's solid shoulder. "You'll get a better job; meanwhile this is honest work."

Leo's eyes met Alvaro's for a split second of total rapport. "I know. I just wish it paid as well as dishonest work."

"The money's not worth it," Alvaro said. "Right?"

"Right." Leo sighed and trudged through the roll-up door of the garage.

Kiki's eyes followed Leo. "You don't think he'd ever go back to being a package boy for those drug dealers, do you?"

"Not a chance," Alvaro said, putting his arm around Kiki's shoulders as they walked away. "If anyone's going back to a life of crime, it's me. I need the money a lot more than Leo does."

"Shut up!" Kiki poked Alvaro in the side. "You made a promise too."

"I remember, and I'm keeping my promise just like Leo."

"Good." Kiki paused. "Listen, man, if you really need money—"

"Forget it. I'll get by until we win first prize at the festival."

"Splitting fifteen hundred dollars three ways won't get you far."

"No shit. You know I'm talking about the talent scouts that are going to be fighting over us."

"We're good," Kiki said as they reached the bus stop. "But I still think we need something more to get a contract, something that'll blow people away, something… original."

"I've been working on some steps based on kickboxing."

"Lame. Dancing and martial arts have been combined before hundreds, maybe thousands, of times."

"Then you think of something," Alvaro said as the bus pulled up to the curb.

Kiki dug his bus pass from his pocket, waving at the driver to wait a second. "I'll try to get inspired," he said. "See you in school, cool."

"See you," Alvaro said as Kiki bounded onto the bus. As the big vehicle drove away leaving behind a cloud of diesel fumes, Alvaro started jogging home. He had a fair distance to cover and plenty of time to think about the dance routine, but he kept picturing Cande looking up at him as he bandaged his wound. Dark gray with a blue tint. That's what color Cande's eyes were. The color of a stormy sky. "Oh man," Alvaro breathed as he realized he couldn't get the new kid out of his mind. "I really don't need this right now."

Pushing himself harder, he ran until the burning of his muscles occupied his thoughts. After checking on his mother, he collapsed on his narrow bed, gazing up at the ceiling, his chest heaving as he panted for breath. His eyes followed the familiar road map of the cracks in the plaster as his breathing slowed, and his mind began to wander. When it became obvious that he couldn't banish the new kid from his thoughts, he gave in and gave his imagination free rein. He pretended that Cande hadn't stopped with hinting that he liked guys. He pictured Cande kneeling in front of him. Imagined Cande unzipping him. Alvaro's hand slipped under the waistband of his trousers, pretending it was Cande's hand stroking his stiffening cock. Closing his eyes, he painted a mental portrait of Cande looking up at him, perfect lips wrapped around his cock. He gasped, buttocks rising from the mattress as his climax burst in him like a warehouse-worth of fireworks. Shuddering through the powerful orgasm, he dropped back onto the bed, holding tight to his cock. "*Jesus,*" he breathed as the ripples of pleasure began to recede. He lay unmoving for several minutes before he peeled off his jeans and tossed them onto the pile of dirty laundry. A shower would be good, but he was feeling too lethargic to do anything about it just yet. A mental image of Cande wet and naked was the last thing he remembered before he woke the next morning.

chapter Two

"HEY, guys!" Eligio got off his bike and started walking it next to Alvaro, Kiki, and Leo.

"Beat it," Leo said automatically.

"We're all going the same way," Eligio said. "It's a public sidewalk. Why can't I walk with you?"

"You're causing a sharp drop in our coolness quotient," Kiki said.

"I'm wearing jeans," Eligio pointed out. "Let me hang out with you and watch you practice."

"No way," Leo said. "I have the afternoon off, and I'm not spending it with you."

"Ah, who cares?" Alvaro said. "He can come watch us practice if he wants to." He ignored Leo and Kiki's incredulous stares and kept walking. Candelario Carlisle hadn't been in school today, and Alvaro couldn't seem to concentrate on anything else.

"Okay, but you have to bring drinks for everyone," Leo told Eligio.

"No problem," Eligio said. "I'll meet you guys at the garage." Turning his bicycle around, Eligio pedaled off to his family's small convenience store.

"He looks like a giraffe that lost his training wheels," Kiki observed.

"I can't believe you told the nerd he could hang with us," Leo said to Alvaro.

"He's not hurting anybody," Alvaro said. "Cut the kid some slack. You weren't always Mr. Cool, you know."

"The hell I wasn't," Leo said as he pushed open the gate to the garage's back lot. "At least with the garage closed, we won't have my coworkers making fun of us."

"They're just jealous," Kiki said, pulling out his phone to check the time. "Let's get started. I have to be on time for dinner tonight."

"What's the occasion and is that a new phone?" Alvaro asked.

"Yeah, check this out," Kiki said. "It's the latest model, a present from my parents. I suspect it's supposed to cushion whatever bombshell they're laying on me at dinner."

"I didn't know they were in town."

"They got in late last night." Kiki yawned. "Woke me up to give me presents like I'm nine years old or something. It probably came from the duty-free shop."

"It's a nice phone," Alvaro said as Leo turned up the boom box. "Ready to dance?"

"I thought you'd never ask," Kiki said as he sprang to his feet.

The three young men lined up and rehearsed the dance routine that they'd put together step by step. Every now and then, one of them would pause and show the other two something that had occurred to him, and they'd incorporate it or vote it down. Eligio returned, but they ignored him for almost half an hour until Kiki declared he was dying of thirst.

"I got flavored sparkling water, hope that's okay," Eligio said as he handed out bottles. "Guess who I saw at the store? The new kid."

"Cande Carlisle?" Alvaro asked immediately.

"Settle down, Romeo," Kiki said.

Alvaro faked a yawn. "I don't know what you mean by that."

"Please," Leo snorted, falling in with the ragging. "I can't remember the last time I saw you this excited. You've got a crush on the new guy."

"You're both delusional," Alvaro said.

"It's okay, you know," Kiki said, putting a hand on Alvaro's shoulder. "I won't think anything different about you. You'll always be my good friend." He grinned. "No matter who you sleep with."

"*Chingate*," Alvaro said affectionately.

"I'm only half joking," Kiki said. "Anyone that can cook like Carlisle is a catch."

"What are you talking about?" Eligio asked suspiciously.

"Never mind," Alvaro said. "That's a conversation for another day. What did you think of our dancing?"

"You're really good," Eligio said. "But I've seen at least three other formation dance groups that are just about as good."

"I told you," Kiki sighed. "We need something to set us apart."

"We need some flashy costumes," Leo said. "Man, if we only had some money."

"Usually, I'd be the first to agree," Kiki said, "but we'll need more than that."

"You should sing while you dance," Eligio said. "Not that you have time to learn a song before the festival."

"What makes you think any of us can sing anyway?" Alvaro asked.

"You know Leo can sing; he sings all the time," Eligio said.

"That's true," Alvaro said. "You really have a good voice, Leo. I'm no singer, though."

"You do everything well," Eligio said confidently. "If Kiki has a decent voice, you could harmonize. I could help you with the arrangements."

"How do you know so much about it?" Leo asked.

"I've been in chorus since second grade. I know about harmony and phrasing and arrangements and—"

"Alvaro," Leo interrupted Eligio's stream of words, "are we taking advice from sophomores now?"

Alvaro wasn't listening. He was looking past Eligio at the chain link fence. Eligio turned and waved at the young man standing by the gate. "Sorry," Eligio said. "I forgot to say that I mentioned to Cande that he could stop by if he wanted."

"It's okay," Alvaro said and raised his voice. "Cande! Come on in."

Kiki exchanged a glance with Leo. Alvaro's voice had an upbeat tone that was all too rare these days. If Cande Carlisle was the cause of Alvaro's lighter mood, then Kiki would give the new kid some leeway. Leo's wink told Kiki that Leo was also willing to reserve judgment.

"You know my friends, don't you?" Alvaro said when Cande reached them. "Have you been grocery shopping?" He nodded at the large bag Cande held in front of him.

Cande nodded. "I thought you might have finished the beans and rice by now so I bought stuff to make a stew."

"Really? Mama asked for some of your beans and rice this morning. It's the first time in years that she's been interested in food."

"That was good *frijoles*," Kiki said. "It cleared my sinuses and everything else."

"Are we going to practice anymore today?" Leo asked. "Or are we going to have home ec class?"

"What about this singing idea?" Kiki said. "I want to hear more about it."

"You're singers?" Cande said. "I thought Eligio said you were dancers."

"We're dancers," Alvaro said. "But Eligio thinks we should sing too."

"Eligio thinks everyone should sing," Cande said. "He doesn't seem to realize that not everyone has a great voice like he does."

"He does?" Kiki said.

Cande nodded. "He's in advanced chorus with me even though he's just a sophomore, and he's the best singer in the group."

"This is a practical joke," Leo said. "If the nerd could sing, we'd know about it."

"Let's hear you," Alvaro said, pointing to Eligio.

"In front of you guys?" Eligio shook his head.

"Come on." Cande nudged Eligio with his elbow. "Don't be modest. You're good. Just close your eyes like you do when Luisa Hernandez looks at you in class."

Leo's jaw dropped as Eligio sang the first line of a song that was on the radio all the time. By the time Eligio got to the end of the verse, everyone's mouth was hanging open. When Leo joined him, adding a soaring high harmony on the chorus, the other three were astonished at how much it sounded like the recording. Leo smiled at Kiki and made a beckoning gesture. Kiki began to sing along on the second chorus in a rich baritone that gave depth to the harmony. Alvaro joined in, singing in unison with Kiki, and by the third chorus each had found his part and was having fun with it. Leo and Kiki were even doing a few steps of their dance routine when Cande impulsively added his voice to the mix. In a few seconds, the new kid was singing alone as the others stopped to listen. Cande faltered to a stop under their stares. "Sorry, I didn't mean to butt in."

"Damn," Kiki said. "I've never heard anyone sing like that."

"You're all just as good," Cande said.

Leo made a noise with his tongue and lips. "Yeah, right."

"You've got wonderful voices," Cande said. "Tell them, Eligio."

"It's true," Eligio said. "You guys are good. You're naturals."

"Maybe we've got good voices," Kiki said, "but we're not trained singers. You and Cande sound amazing." He paused. "Seriously, I've never heard a voice like Cande's, on the radio maybe, but not in, you know, real life."

"I can teach you how to project your voice like that," Eligio said.

"The very notion of *you* teaching us anything is fundamentally wrong," Kiki said. "But stranger things have happened. Alvaro?"

"I think we should give singing a try," Alvaro said, his eyes on Cande. "You want to give us a hand?"

"I don't know," Cande said. "I'm already cooking for you, and now you want singing lessons? Where will it end?"

"That's up to you," Alvaro said.

"Hey, no flirting during work time," Kiki said.

"I should get going anyway," Alvaro said. "Mama's been alone long enough."

"Okay," Kiki said. "See you tomorrow."

"See you in school," Leo said as he walked toward his room above the garage.

"See you tomorrow, Eligio," Alvaro said as he steered Cande out the gate.

"See you tomorrow." Eligio beamed as he hopped on his bicycle and pedaled away.

On the sidewalk, Kiki turned to go to his bus stop and paused when he realized Alvaro wasn't at his side. He turned and saw his friend watching Cande walk in the other direction. He stomped on a small flame of jealousy and called to Alvaro. "Take off, man. I can find my way to the bus by myself."

Alvaro waved a goodbye over his shoulder and hurried to catch up with Cande. "Thanks for waiting," he said sarcastically as he took the bag of groceries from the other boy.

"I can carry it. Also, I know the way to your place, and I thought you might want to talk to your friend without me around."

"Why would you think that?"

"I don't know. I didn't do a study on it or anything; I just felt like I was intruding."

"You're not. I want you around."

"Maybe you should ask Kiki if he wants me around."

"Maybe you should just say what's on your mind."

"I just don't want to cause trouble for anybody."

"Don't sweat it. So… what's in the bag?" Alvaro looked down.

"Just the usual stuff for making stew."

"My usual stuff is a big can and a can opener."

Cande rolled his eyes. "No wonder you think my cooking's good. I'm saving you from bland food."

"And it's very nice of you," Alvaro said as they entered his apartment. "I'll pay you back for the groceries, of course."

"I like to cook." Cande shrugged. "And it gives me somewhere to be."

"Your home life's not so good?"

Cande shrugged again as he lined ingredients up on the counter. "No one has a perfect life," he said. "Do you have a really big pot?"

When the stew was simmering on the stove, Cande went up to the roof to watch Alvaro practice kickboxing. Alvaro insisted on showing Cande a couple of moves, and Cande ended up hitting the ground on his back with the wind knocked out of him. "Sorry," Alvaro said, offering his hand. He hauled the other boy up until they were standing chest to chest. Cande swallowed hard as Alvaro's face came closer. He couldn't breathe, and every nerve was singing like the rim of a crystal wineglass. He closed his eyes and felt something as soft as petals brush his mouth before pressing harder. With a yelp, he jumped backward, his fingers going to his split lip. Raising his head, he met Alvaro's surprised gaze.

"What was that?" Alvaro asked.

"My lip's sore," Cande lisped.

"No, I meant… did you feel…?" Alvaro let out a big breath. "Sorry. I just really wanted to kiss you."

"I wanted you to kiss me; I think."

"Really?" Alvaro leaned toward Cande again.

"You can't!" Cande jumped away again.

"Why not? You just said you wanted me to. And the other day, you kind of said you thought you might like guys."

"I know and I do, but that doesn't mean I'm going to do anything about it." Cande's eyes slid to the side. "The world's a hard place when you're different; it just isn't smart to be gay."

"Okay, I get it. You're scared."

"Damn right, I'm scared. Look at me. I'm exactly the kind of guy that bullies like to pick on. Maybe if I were you I'd be braver, but I'm not you."

"I'll protect you."

"Yeah, that makes it all better." Cande shook his head. "Just forget about it, okay?"

"How? You're under my skin, in my head. I can smell your hair in my sleep. I've got a constant hard-on and—"

Cande smiled. "I knew you'd eventually get to the point."

"It's not like that," Alvaro protested, and then he continued with a sheepish look. "Well, it is like that, but I don't want you just for sex."

"What else could you want me for? We just met two days ago. You don't know me at all."

"That's crap. I know you enough. I know you're scared. I can tell you've been hurt. I bet you want to be loved. So I know how you feel and I know how I feel. What else is there?"

"I… I can't," Cande said.

"Never?"

"I don't know. Never is a long time."

"So there's a possibility?"

"The merest. It's just too dangerous."

"I wish I could say that I don't understand." Alvaro ran a hand over Cande's glossy red-amber hair. "I'm not going to give up, though."

"I didn't think you would."

"Is that okay with you?"

"I can't stop you."

"You won't be annoyed?"

"I won't be annoyed." Cande paused. "Unless my stew burns," he said as he hurried to the stairs.

Alvaro followed Cande to the kitchen and watched him add more cilantro to the pot. His eyes lingered on the other young man's slim fingers handling the big knife so competently, lingered on the slope of his neck and back as he leaned over the cutting board, on the curves of those perfect lips. "Can you dance?" he asked abruptly.

"I don't know."

"What do you mean you don't know?"

"I've never tried it."

"You're kidding. Not even by yourself in your room?"

"Well, yeah, but not much, and I have no idea what it looked like."

"You're kidding," Alvaro said again. "I spent hours dancing in front of the mirror in my room." He grinned. "I still do."

"I guess I'm just weird."

"No you're not," Alvaro said quickly.

Cande gave him an incredulous look over his shoulder.

"Okay, you're a little weird," Alvaro said. "But that makes you interesting."

"You're the first person who's ever said that to me. Interesting… I like it. It sounds a lot better than weird or freak or retard."

"Who called you that?"

"You mean just since I've been at this school?" Cande smiled. "Forget about it. Some people need to feel like they're better than someone else. Fighting them is pointless. Ignoring them drives them crazy."

"Why would you want to make them crazy? Give them a good smack the first time they act up, and they'll think twice the next time."

"I'm sure that works for you, but I'm not your size, and I don't know kickboxing."

"I'll teach you."

"You're assuming I want to learn. Honestly, it looks like hard work."

"It is, but it's worth it. I'll teach you to dance at the same time."

"I don't think so."

"Come on. You have to let me do something to pay you back for cooking."

"I'll think about it." Cande picked up his backpack.

"Do you have to go?"

"Yeah. Someone was missing at bed check last night, so curfew's been moved up a couple of hours."

"Curfew? Bed check?"

"I live in a foster home right now with four other guys."

"Sounds more like prison."

"It's not exactly homey, but it's better than the street."

"I thought you said you were adopted."

"I was, but it didn't work out. If we're done with my history, I should get going."

"Wait. Why weren't you in school today?"

"I just didn't feel like going."

"Are you sure? 'Cause if you're nervous about running into Chuy and his pals, I'll walk with you to your classes."

Cande shook his head, but he was smiling. "You would be the best boyfriend ever."

"Ah, so you finally noticed." Alvaro nodded, adopting a sly expression. "My deviously clever plan is working perfectly."

"You're seriously deranged," Cande said as he walked to the door.

"Do you find that attractive?"

Cande laughed as he left the apartment and closed the door behind him. Alvaro stood unmoving for several heartbeats with the sound of Cande's laugh ringing in his ears. He loved the way the sound burst from Cande's throat, as if Cande was surprised to be laughing. He liked the way it made him feel to know he'd made Cande happy. He wanted to keep making Cande happy.

"I'm screwed," he said as he started down the hall to his mother's room. "A hopeless case. I cannot afford to do this right now. I've got too much going on." He stopped at the bedroom door and leaned his forehead against the wooden panel. *But he smells so good, and everything he does makes me want him, makes me want to protect him, make sure he's okay.* "Damn it," he swore under his breath as he opened the door. He spent a couple of hours watching television and having dinner with his mother. Tuning out the sparkly silliness of the game shows she favored, Alvaro did some more thinking about the Cande situation.

He couldn't deny the strong physical attraction he felt for the new kid. He'd had those feelings for boys as well as girls for as long as he could remember, and he'd experimented with both, but he'd never felt this strongly about it before. He knew it would be wise to stay away from Cande, but he wanted to be with him more than he'd ever wanted anything. He also knew that his desire would win out over wisdom. He was being stupid, walking off the cliff with his eyes wide open, giving something for nothing like the fool he was under his façade of coolness. Because beneath all his reasoning and all his lust was the simple fact that Cande was his; he hadn't doubted that since he'd first seen him. They belonged together, whether as friends, brothers, or lovers. Even if Cande never slept with him or called him his best friend, Alvaro would still feel this way and want to do whatever he could to make Cande's life better. "I really hope this doesn't turn out to be a disaster," he said under his breath.

Alvaro's mother turned from the screen, and her gaze fell on her son's drooping head. She reached out and put her hand on his springy black hair. Alvaro looked up in surprise, but she had already gone back to watching television. He took her hand between both of his and held it until the show was over. "Good night, Mama," he said, leaning over to kiss her forehead before leaving the room.

He was able to resist jerking off to images of Cande at least until he got to the shower. As he was leaning against the plastic wall with his spent cock in his hand, the hot water bouncing off his skin, and the strongest orgasm he'd ever had reverberating in every cell, he finally stopped worrying about the Cande situation. He was going to stop over-thinking things in general and see how that worked. Brooding certainly wasn't making anything any better. Maybe he should be more like Kiki and just take it a little easier. "Yeah. Sure I will," he said sarcastically as he turned off the water.

chapter *Three*

"YOU'D better have my money today, asshole." Chuy Alvarez gave Cande a shove.

Cande held tight to the strap of his backpack as one of Chuy's friends pushed him from behind. "I don't have anything for you. Please move out of the way. The bell's going to ring any minute."

"Do I care?" Chuy sneered, slapping Cande lightly across both cheeks. "If you don't want me to hit you a lot harder, you'll get smart and hand over some money, *maricon*."

"I don't have any money. I get my lunch with a meal ticket. Do you get it now?"

"You're on welfare?" Chuy smirked. "It figures. What a loser."

"Leave me alone," Cande said as he wrenched free of the hand on his elbow.

"You need to learn a little respect, faggot," Chuy said. The sound of his palm striking the other boy's cheek was loud in the space between the two buildings. He drew back his hand again and it was taken in an iron grip.

"Are you just plain stupid?" Alvaro asked.

Chuy tried to yank his hand free, and then he tried again. The strain was evident in his voice when he spoke. "Let me go, dumbfuck. Or my boys will destroy you."

"If you keep pulling, you're going to dislocate something," Alvaro said calmly. "If your boys take another step toward me, I'll make sure you break something."

"Let me go and they'll let your boyfriend go."

"Deal." Alvaro flung Chuy away and took hold of Cande's upper arm. Pulling Cande away from Chuy's gang, Alvaro moved to stand in front of him. "Since you're so slow," he said to Chuy, "I'm going to explain it to you in small words. Cande Carlisle is with me. If you ask him for money again or otherwise fuck with him, I'll end you. *Comprende?*"

"You think I'm scared of you?"

"Yes, I do, but only because I've kicked your ass before and it was so easy."

"Why don't you take your boyfriend and go before we have to dig a couple of shallow graves?"

Alvaro blinked. "Did you just threaten to kill my boyfriend? You really *are* stupid. Now I have to kill you to make sure you don't kill him."

"It was a figure of speech," Chuy said quickly.

"Like 'boyfriend' is a figure of speech?" Cande asked.

Alvaro barely kept the smile from his face as he gave Chuy another warning. "If you really think Cande is my boyfriend then you should be extra careful not to piss him off. Now scamper. You're blocking the alley."

"So you've saved me again," Cande said as he and Alvaro watched Chuy's gang walk away.

"Why didn't you wait for me to walk with you? You know Chuy's got it in for you."

"That's Chuy's problem." Cande slung his backpack over his shoulder.

"Want to eat lunch with me?"

"Sure."

"Want to come over after school?"

"You finished the stew already? I made enough for a week!"

"For your dancing lessons," Alvaro said. "You can go to practice with me too."

"Are you sure it's okay with your friends?"

"I'll ask them, but why wouldn't it be okay?"

Cande shrugged and changed the subject. "It's kind of nice having a hero."

"Yeah? Aren't you worried that people will get the wrong idea?" Alvaro teased.

"After the last few days...." Cande paused, rethinking his words. "I just feel like I can trust you. I feel like I can believe you when you say that you'll be there for me."

"I *will* be there for you." Alvaro realized he was offering Cande everything with no guarantee that he'd get anything in return, but he didn't care. There wasn't much he could do about it anyway. He accepted that he was head over heels for this odd boy and focused on doing what he could to make Cande feel the same way about him. He was well aware that homosexuals weren't welcome in his neighborhood, but he trusted in his strength and his friends to save him if he got into that kind of trouble.

"It... means a lot to me." Cande ducked his head. "To have a real friend, I mean."

"Me too. My friends are everything to me." Alvaro paused. "You understand that I feel more for you than friendship though, right?"

Cande nodded. "You've made it very clear, don't worry."

"If all I'm doing is bugging you, let me know, okay? But if you're at all interested, could you give me just one little sign? *Por favor, gracias.*"

Cande said something under his breath and then raised his voice. "I want you around," he said, quoting Alvaro's words. "But you can't be acting all gay with me in public. That shit will get you fucked up; believe me. There are a fuck of a lot of queer-hating assholes in this world."

"Good enough." Alvaro hid his shock at the sudden spate of profanity. Not that cussing shocked him, but it was the first time he'd heard Cande swear like that. He wanted to ask what had happened to put that harsh bitterness in Cande's melodic voice, but they came around a corner and joined a stream of students headed for the cafeteria. Cande wouldn't let Alvaro stand in line with him, sending him outside to meet his friends. Alvaro left reluctantly, glancing back several times as he joined Leo, Kiki, and Eligio. Eligio handed Alvaro a bag lunch as Alvaro sat on the grass between Kiki and Leo. Alvaro held up the bag, looking at the greasy paper. "Is this one of your mama's chorizo empanadas?"

Eligio nodded as he looked at the soggy bag. "I guess it got a little smashed in my backpack."

"Don't worry about it," Alvaro said. "It'll taste just as good."

"We were just talking about what song we should sing," Kiki said as Alvaro devoured his food. "Since we've apparently decided to add something new to our act at the last minute."

"We need the perfect song to go with our dancing," Leo put in. "And it shouldn't be too hard to learn fast."

Eligio nodded. "Something that people know but haven't heard so many times that they're sick of it."

"Good point, Elly," Alvaro said.

"Elly!" Leo howled as he broke into laughter over the new nickname.

"It's perfect!" Kiki said, catching Leo's giggles. "Elly. It's so cute!"

"Cut it out. You don't hear me calling you Leocita," Eligio said.

"Because you wouldn't dare," Leo stopped laughing abruptly.

"Children, please," Alvaro said. "Can we talk about something constructive?" He caught each of the other boys' eyes in turn. "I want to invite Cande to perform with us."

Leo's mouth fell open. "Two weeks from the festival and you want to bring in a new guy? Well, I'm not splitting my share of the prize money."

"Two new guys," Alvaro said, patting Eligio's shoulder.

"So now we're a quintet?" Kiki said quietly.

"Only if we all agree. Just think about it," Alvaro said as Cande arrived. "Hi. Have a seat."

"Yeah. Have a seat right here," Kiki said, making room between him and Alvaro.

Alvaro reacted to Kiki's tone by giving him a disbelieving look. "If I want you to move, I'll ask you," he said. He turned to Leo. "Move over."

"Ha ha ha," Leo said as he stood up. "I want another soda anyway. Elly! Go get me a soda."

Eligio pouted but left with some of Leo's money as Leo started doing a few dance steps on the grass. Kiki looked up and made an approving noise. "That's really smooth, man," he said.

"I saw an old Michael Jackson video at the pool hall last night," Leo said. "It kind of impressed me the way it did when I was a little kid."

"He was the business all right," Kiki said. "Too bad he got mixed up in funny business."

"Maybe we should do something really old school," Alvaro said. "I'm not saying we should go out and do 'Thriller', but something cool and funky like that would suit us."

"No doubt," Leo said, dipping in a deep knee bend to rub his butt against Kiki's back before rising up again. "We're bringing the heat with this routine."

Kiki reached up and smacked Leo on the ass. "Yeah, but remember to keep it to a simmer. This is a family event."

Cande got up to throw his trash away, and Alvaro's eyes followed him to the bin and back. "I have to go," Cande said. "The music building's on the other side of campus."

"I'll go with you," Alvaro said as he got to his feet.

"See you at practice?" Kiki asked.

"Of course. Let's all try and think of a few good songs, and we'll pick one at practice. We're not losing anything by trying it. If we can't learn a song in time, we'll go with our original act."

Leo and Kiki watched Alvaro hurry after Cande. "Well, you were right," Leo said as he began to unlace his studded leather wrist band.

"Before you hand that over," Kiki said, "are you sure you don't want a little more proof?"

Leo shook his head. "I don't need any more proof that Alvaro's thinking with his dick again. The wrist band is yours. If you'd lost the bet, I'd've taken your phone." He sat down next to Kiki. "I'm just surprised that it's a guy... even one as pretty as Carlisle."

Kiki snorted. "You remember when we met? The summer before freshman year?"

Leo made the same snorting noise. "Yeah, I vaguely recall it. It was only three years ago."

"Remember how Alvaro had a new best friend every other day? You remember those guys, right? Alvaro would bring them to the beach with him at night. They never looked like surfers or skaters like the rest of us that hung out down there. They looked like... models or actors or something and had names like Justin, Jason, and Cody."

"I don't remember every jerk that hung out at the bonfire that summer. We weren't friends yet, anyway."

"*We* weren't friends yet, but you and Alvaro were. That's probably why I heard the gossip and you didn't. People figured you'd kick their ass if they called Alvaro a fag in front of you."

Leo raised an eyebrow. "I just figured those guys were white-bread rich kids that wanted to pretend they were street for a night. I just assumed Alvaro was letting them pay for his good times, but if you tell me that he fooled around with every one of them that summer... well, you've never lied to me, so I guess I believe you. But come on, he fooled around with an awful lot of girls too."

"Yeah, I know; just about all of them. I was in love with Brandi Herrero. Then I found out from her best friend that she was only dating me because I hung out with Alvaro's crowd sometimes. She had a huge crush on him."

"Who didn't?" Leo shrugged. "Is that why you dumped her?"

"Knowing she was using me to get to Alvaro kind of took the fun out of it."

Leo nodded. "I could never figure out why you blew her off. She was the hottest chick on the beach, man. I can still see her in that white string bikini. I would've loved a shot at her."

"She was fourteen."

"We were all fourteen," Leo said wryly.

Kiki chuckled. "Right." He looked over his left shoulder and back at Leo. "Does it bother you that Alvaro's, you know, bisexual?"

"I don't know for sure that he is until he tells me."

"But you must think he's up to something with Cande, or you wouldn't have handed over your beloved wrist band, which you can have back, by the way." Kiki threw the studded leather bracer into Leo's lap. "It looks a lot better on you."

"Cool," Leo said. "And about Alvaro's sex life…. I know we're supposed to be macho and everything and hate *maricons*, but Alvaro Torres is a stand-up guy, you know? He didn't turn his back on me when I got in trouble. He helped me get out and helped me keep my family from finding out about how bad it really was. So I say if he wants to date grandmothers, hookers, or pretty boys, then that's his business. It doesn't change who he is." Leo paused. "Although, if he wanted to date Elly, I'd have to draw the line."

"What are you guys talking about?" Eligio heard his new nickname as he trotted up with Leo's soda.

Leo looked at Kiki over the rim of the can and both smiled. "Never mind," Kiki said. "It would just confuse you."

Eligio opened his mouth, but the bell rang. Leo and Kiki strolled away, leaving the younger boy with a puzzled frown on his face. "See you at practice," Eligio called out. When the other two kept walking, Eligio locked up his bike and headed off to class.

"YOU got it?" Alvaro shouted over the rooftop wind, looking at Cande on his right.

Cande brushed some strands of hair away from his mouth as he answered. "I think so. Once I repeat it several million times I'm sure I'll have it."

Alvaro grinned. Cande was a good student, and his off-hand, self-mocking sense of humor was slowly revealing itself. "You've learned a lot in two hours. Come on. Let's go meet the others and show them."

"Are you sure?"

Alvaro cocked his head to one side and regarded Cande somberly. "Do you want to do this or not?"

Cande nodded, his eyes widening as though the fact was an abrupt revelation to him. "Yeah, I do. It's not something I ever imagined myself doing, but I've had more fun in the last few hours than I've had in the last few years. I love singing, always have, but I think I love dancing just as much. How weird is that?"

"It's not weird at all. You're going to be really good at this; I can tell. It won't be that hard to teach you the steps of one specific dance over the next week, but teaching all of us to sing and dance at the same time is going to take some work."

"Why worry about that until you talk to your friends?"

Alvaro took Cande's hand and raised it to shoulder level, interlacing their fingers. "*Our* friends," he said, meeting the other boy's eyes. "I'd really like to kiss you."

Cande's tongue came out to moisten his lips. "I guess that would be all right." He glanced around. "No one can see us here, right?"

Alvaro didn't wait for Cande to talk himself out of it. Wrapping his arm around Cande's shoulders, he pressed their lips together in a kiss with more passion than finesse. Cande's fingers tightened on Alvaro's as his free hand settled on Alvaro's back. Alvaro's tongue swiped across Cande's lower lip, and he let his hand slide down Cande's back to the top curve of his butt. With gentle pressure, Alvaro brought the lower halves of their bodies into contact. As their crotches touched, Cande broke the kiss, opening his eyes to look into Alvaro's dark gaze.

"You've got a hard-on," Cande said.

"I get hard just thinking about you. Kissing is bound to have an effect."

"Why do I torture you like this?" Cande sighed. "It's not right to lead you on."

"I'm not complaining. I like that we're taking it slow."

"You're used to things happening fast, I guess."

Alvaro shrugged. "Whatever. I'm glad we're going slow."

"Where do you see us going exactly?"

"I'm hoping you'll suddenly realize you're crazy about me. We'll make out until we have to stop for food, and then we'll really get busy. Rinse and repeat for the rest of our lives."

"You want to marry me, Alvaro Torres?" Cande chuckled.

"Sure." Alvaro said immediately. Then he paused a moment before asking, "Can we do that?"

Cande shook his head. "Not legally, but we can have some kind of ceremony and promise to be together forever." He looked down suddenly. "I mean if we felt that way some day, you know?"

Alvaro smiled at the top of Cande's head. "Sure. I know what you mean. Come on," he tugged on Cande's hand. "We're going to be late. That won't impress anyone."

"THAT'S horrible," Kiki said. "Are you doing an impression of a dying orangutan?"

"Orangutan?" Leo said. "I was thinking he looked like a grasshopper on a hot sidewalk."

Eligio glared at his critics, but kept dancing until the song was over.

"Come on, you guys," Alvaro said. "It wasn't that bad. You did fine, Elly; you'll pick it up fast. Okay, Cande, show them what you learned."

Cande nodded and went to stand in the center of the concrete slab. Leo hit the music, and Cande began to move. When the song ended, there was a spontaneous burst of applause.

"Damn!" Leo said. "Are you sure you never danced before?"

"Yeah, be honest," Kiki said. "You must have had some training."

"Only in singing," Cande said. "Varo's just a really good teacher."

Kiki smirked. "Oh, I'm sure *Varo* has a lot to teach you." Alvaro shot Kiki a sharp look, and Kiki added, "About dancing."

Cande looked confused for about two seconds and then burst out laughing. "This is too funny! Varo, you don't have to protect my delicate self from your friends. I'll bet that a few days ago, you would've laughed at Kiki's remark."

Kiki raised his eyebrows at Alvaro. Alvaro had the grace to look embarrassed. "Sorry, bro," he mumbled. "I was being a jerk."

"We're cool," Kiki said, punching Alvaro lightly on the shoulder. "Know what else is cool? Your new boyfriend. Why didn't I ever think to call you Varo? It's a lot cooler than Alvaro."

"You really think so?" Alvaro put an arm around Kiki and pretended to inspect Cande from head to toe. "He's kind of skinny."

Leo chuckled. "And he's a flake."

Kiki tilted his head. "Plus he's just so ugly he makes my eyes hurt."

Alvaro nodded. "True. Do you think we can give him a makeover?"

"He'll need some jeans," Eligio spoke up. Everyone turned to him, and he looked around in embarrassment. "But I know jeans are expensive and none of us is rich." He paused again. "Except for Kiki maybe, but we can't expect him to...." Eligio's stream of nervous chatter trailed off.

Kiki slapped Cande on the shoulder. "He can borrow a pair of mine until he gets some. We look like we wear the same size."

"My big sister just got a new pair because she outgrew her old ones," Eligio said. "I bet they'd fit." He turned red when everyone started laughing. "I didn't mean—"

"I know you didn't mean anything by it except a kind offer," Cande said. "I'd really like to join your group," he went on. "I promise I'll work hard to learn to dance."

"Should we vote on it now?" Leo asked.

"I vote yes," Kiki said. "Whether we vote now or later."

"Me too," Leo said. "I assume we don't even have to bother asking Alvaro."

Alvaro grinned. "That just leaves Elly."

"What?" Eligio looked utterly astonished. "I get a vote?"

"You've been a junior member long enough. What do you say?"

"Yes! Of course!"

"Then it's settled," Alvaro said. "We're a party of five."

"Hell yes! Party!" Leo held up his palm for Alvaro to slap.

"I like that," Kiki said. "It wouldn't be a bad name: Party of Five. And we can't exactly call ourselves the Three of Hearts anymore, can we?"

By the time practice ended, the boys had settled on calling themselves Party of Five, chosen a song from the year four of them were born in, and integrated the two new members into the first steps of the dance routine. The owner of the garage came out to bitch about the yard light being a waste of electricity, and the young men scattered. Leo went up to his room, making a rude gesture behind his boss's back. Eligio walked his bike next to Kiki until they got to the bus stop, and Eligio rode away toward home. Alvaro took Cande's hand and pulled him down an alleyway to a parallel street with a lot less traffic. There were more homes than storefronts and a few trees among the streetlights.

"Can I walk you home?" Alvaro asked.

"No!" Cande said immediately.

"Take it easy. I didn't ask for a blow job."

"Sorry. I just don't want you to see where I live."

"It can't be much worse than my place. We barely have room to turn around."

"Just drop it, okay?"

"Okay. Can I put my arm around you?"

Cande looked sideways at Alvaro. "What kind of question is that? You've been all over me since we met. Why even ask?"

"Okay, I deserved that. I *have* been pawing you." He paused. "It's just that… when I saw Chuy's hands on you… well, it made me think about what you said, about not wanting to be forced into anything. So I thought that from now on, I'd ask before I did anything."

Cande stopped at the corner and looked up at Alvaro. "If it bothered me, I'd tell you to stop."

Alvaro licked his lips. "So, let me see if I understand. I can touch you until you say no?"

Cande nodded and boldly took Alvaro's hand as he crossed the intersection. Alvaro reversed his grip, wrapping his fingers around Cande's as they walked down the deserted street. Everyone else was inside at dinner, and by the time they reached the walkway over the railroad tracks, Alvaro and Cande felt like the only two people in the world.

Alvaro stopped halfway and put his arms loosely around Cande's waist, his hands resting on the swell of Cande's butt. Cande put his head on Alvaro's shoulder, hiding his face in the curve of Alvaro's neck. They stood that way for a long time until Alvaro broke the silence. "This feels so good."

Cande nodded. "I actually feel… happy."

Alvaro's arms tightened around Cande, hugging him close as he kissed his forehead. "I wish we could feel like this forever."

Cande shivered. "If we fell from here, we'd hit the electrified rail and be killed instantly."

"What? Why would you say something like that?"

"We'd be together forever. Out of the reach of anyone that wanted to hurt us. And this would be the last thing we ever felt so we'd feel this way forever."

"That's very romantic, but a little dark for me."

Cande lifted his face to the moonlight. "I was kidding," he said.

"It didn't sound like it." Alvaro brushed the heavy bangs off Cande's forehead. "You don't really think about killing yourself, do you?"

"Not anymore."

Alvaro's eyes narrowed. "What does that mean?"

"It means I went through a Goth phase before I came here. I can show you pictures of me with long black hair and eyeliner. But since I met you, I don't feel like being depressed all the time."

"Good. You kind of scared me with that talk."

"Forget it, okay? It was just something to say. I forgot that I don't have to put on an act or be all cool with you."

Alvaro rubbed his nose against Cande's. "I love you just the way you are."

"I do sort of wish that you wouldn't use the L word all the time. It's too serious a word to toss around lightly."

"I'm not using it lightly."

"Well it spooks me a little, okay? I just don't think we've known each other long enough to talk about love."

Alvaro mimed zipping his lips. "What's long enough?" he asked. "I'll set my watch."

Cande gave him an air slap. "And stop being so cute all the time. It's hard to resist a man who's not afraid to act silly."

"Why fight it?" Alvaro pulled Cande closer and brought their lips together. He felt Cande's resistance and he almost let him go, but then the soft, soft lips parted for him. Trying to curb his excitement, Alvaro sent his tongue in search of the elusive spicy sweetness that was the taste of Cande. An electric thrill shot through his groin when the other young man responded with a confidence Alvaro hadn't expected. Encouraged, Alvaro grabbed a double handful of Cande's ass and squeezed, fingers sinking into resilient muscle. Cande gasped and drew back as his cheeks were parted. "Sorry," Alvaro said, instantly moving his hands.

"It's okay," Cande said breathlessly. "I just… I gotta go. I'm going to be late."

"I'm really sorry I got carried away. I won't do it again."

"You didn't do anything wrong. Stop apologizing."

"You just get me so excited. Not that it's your fault—"

"It's no one's fault," Cande interrupted. "We have chemistry. It's just the way it is."

"Maybe it's no one's fault that we're attracted to each other, but there has to be a reason that you…." Alvaro's voice trailed off, and he and Cande stared at one another for a long moment.

"I really have to go," Cande said at last.

"I wish you'd let me walk with you."

"What about your mama?"

"Yeah, you're right. She's been alone long enough. See you tomorrow?"

"I hope so." Cande rose on his toes to kiss Alvaro before he turned to go.

Alvaro raised a hand to his mouth as if he could capture the fading feel of Cande's lips against his. "Me and the guys meet here in the morning to walk to school," he called after the other young man.

Cande raised his hand in a wave and kept walking. Alvaro watched until the other boy turned a corner and was gone from sight. His emotions were too big to be contained by anything as frail as human flesh, and he had to run all the way home to bleed off a little of the nervous energy that threatened to burst him. *Cande Carlisle wanted him*, maybe even as much as he wanted Cande Carlisle, but… Cande was still scared.

Alvaro renewed his resolve not to push the other boy too hard or fast. He'd never had the patience for this game before, but it was different now. Something told him Cande was worth waiting for, and he was going to wait, no matter how long it took or how many shades of blue his balls turned. He wasn't going to screw it up by acting like a horn dog, even if he was one. Sex with Cande would no doubt be the most amazing experience this side of heaven, but if it cost Alvaro his friendship, Alvaro knew he'd regret it the rest of his life. What he wanted to have with Cande was worth so much more than a few minutes of pleasure, no matter how good the sex was. "I'm so mature," he muttered sarcastically as he dished up some stew for his mother. Adding a spoonful of rice on the side, he carried a tray into her bedroom. His mood improved when she smiled at him and reached for the spoon without being prompted. "What's on TV tonight?" he asked as he settled into the chair beside the bed.

Halfway through a comedy variety show, the station aired a promotional spot for the upcoming festival and music competition. Alvaro sat forward in his chair, eyes glued to the footage of past performances while the announcer shouted the names of contestants who had gone on to fame and fortune. His mother gazed passively at his rapt expression before she gave her attention back to her food. A few minutes later, Alvaro took her dishes away and went up to the roof to practice. She fell asleep to the rhythm of his steps and dreamed of happier days.

chapter *Four*

CANDE wasn't in school the next day. After the second class, Alvaro took off. He wanted to go look for Cande, but didn't know where to start, so he went home. Even before he got in the door, he knew Cande was there. The smell that filled the house made his mouth water. After checking the pot on the stove and looking in on his mother, Alvaro bounded up the stairs to the roof. It took him a moment to locate Cande stretched out on his stomach like a lizard on the short wall that ran around the edge. As Alvaro's shadow fell over Cande, Cande turned onto his back and gazed up at the clouds.

"I missed you in school," Alvaro said as he sat at Cande's feet.

"I slept in."

Alvaro listened to the wind whistle around the caps of the air vents for a couple of minutes while he studied Cande's face. "You're really special, you know," he said.

"Special," Cande repeated. "That's just a code word for weird, isn't it?"

"You use that word a lot."

"Maybe because I heard it so much when I was little."

"Who called you weird?"

Cande closed his eyes. "I was somewhere between three and four when my second foster parent brought me back to the orphanage. I remember what she said, word for word: 'He doesn't talk. He just watches me with those weird eyes.'"

"Your eyes aren't weird."

"I didn't look like any of the other kids, and no one wanted me."

"Because they're ignorant. I want you." Alvaro took a deep breath. "You don't look like anyone I've ever seen before. You're like something out of a legend where gods and magicians can have any color hair or eyes. You look better than ordinary people."

Cande didn't laugh. "That's—" He swallowed hard. "That's the nicest thing anyone's ever said about me. The kids at the church orphanage made fun of me all the time. They heard one of the priests call me half-breed once and it stuck."

"Assholes."

"I finally got them to stay away from me by telling them I was half-demon and that I'd drink their blood when they fell asleep."

"My little *chupacabra*." Alvaro laughed as he brushed the hair away from Cande's eyes. "There's no one else like you."

"Oh, I'll bet there are lots of people just like me."

"No way. Hey, are you wearing makeup?" Alvaro asked, looking at the powder on his fingers.

"Maybe a little. Just a relapse to my Goth days. Want to kiss me?" Cande lowered his right foot to rest on the roof and opened his arms. Alvaro swung a leg over to straddle the wall and pulled Cande's left leg over his thigh. Leaning forward, Alvaro pressed his crotch to Cande's as he slid an arm under Cande's back to lift him up. Cande interlaced his fingers on Alvaro's nape to pull him down, and their lips met somewhere in the middle. Alvaro leaned harder until Cande's head rested on the wall again. Misty gray eyes gazed up at Alvaro, drawing him ever closer, drawing him into another, deeper kiss that stirred him to his core.

Alvaro shifted and his stiffening cock brushed against a bulge in Cande's trousers. His breath caught in his throat and he sagged, letting most of his weight rest on the other young man. He buried his face in Cande's neck as he rocked forward, rubbing his hardness against Cande's. The wind was a white noise in his ears, drowning out the sounds of the street below, becoming one with Cande's panting breath.

He couldn't stop, and he was thankful that Cande didn't ask him to. Pulsing his hips, he came between one breath and the next, his mouth fastened to the tender skin under Cande's jaw. "*Jesus,*" he groaned as his cum jetted out to soak into his cotton briefs. Cande wrapped his arms around Alvaro's head and held him tight, finger-combing Alvaro's hair. Alvaro was happy to rest there while he absorbed what had happened so very quickly. One second he was kissing Cande, and a minute later, he had jizz cooling off in his underwear. *So much for taking it slow.*

"You okay?" Cande asked.

"Me?" Alvaro raised his head. "I'm not the one being squashed. Go ahead and sit up."

"I'm fine."

"Then sit up so I can hug you."

Cande ducked his head, hiding a smile as he let Alvaro pull him up. Alvaro scooted closer and put an arm around Cande's back. Turning his head, he took Cande's mouth in a sweet kiss as he eased down the zipper of Cande's pants. Cande grabbed Alvaro's wrist, and Alvaro broke the kiss to look into the other boy's eyes.

"You didn't come," Alvaro said softly. "Let me...please."

Cande dropped his eyes and let go of Alvaro's hand. Alvaro leaned in to capture Cande's lips again as his fingers slid under the waistband of Cande's briefs. Cande drew a sharp breath through his nose as Alvaro's long fingers closed around his shaft and squeezed firmly. Alvaro held him tighter, never breaking the kiss as he began to pump his fist. Cande shuddered and spilled thick, hot liquid over Alvaro's knuckles. Alvaro swallowed the little moan that leaked from Cande's mouth when he let go of the sated cock and pulled his hand free. Raising his fingers to his mouth, he licked them clean and then dried them on the tail of his shirt. "Wow," Alvaro said. "I don't know what to say but wow. I didn't expect—"

Cande pushed away from him and stood up. "You should get back to school."

"School?" Alvaro said as if he'd never heard the word before.

"You have two more classes, right?"

"Yeah, but who cares? I want to stay here with you." Alvaro reached out and grabbed Cande by the hips, pulling him onto his lap. "Don't you want me to stay?"

"Come on; I'll go with you. It's time for lunch anyway and I'm hungry," Cande said.

"Why can't we eat here?"

"Because it's not done yet. Let me up."

"Come on, baby." Alvaro kissed the side of Cande's neck. "Can't we just enjoy the moment?"

"Let go," Cande said, pushing away from Alvaro.

Alvaro let him go, getting to his feet as well. "Cande?" He took Cande's hand and swung it gently as he spoke. "You're not mad about what happened, are you?"

Cande shook his head.

"It's really okay that I touched you like that? You didn't seem very sure at first, and now you look kind of mad."

"It's okay."

"Good." Alvaro squeezed Cande's hand. "So it was... okay?"

Cande kept a straight face for a few more seconds before he laughed. "Are you really asking me how good you were?"

"No!" Alvaro said. "Well, maybe. If you had an opinion, I wouldn't mind hearing it."

Cande shook his head. "I don't usually rate hand jobs, but if you insist on knowing then I can tell you that it was transcendent."

"Transcendent?"

"That's right. You have a problem with it?"

"No. No problem. Transcendent, huh?" He followed Cande down the stairs. "It was transcendent for me too." Cande's laugh floated back up to him, and the world was a very sweet place. Now he just needed to look up the word transcendent.

"WHAT do you mean Leo's not joining us?" Eligio put his hands on his hips and stared at Kiki in disbelief. "None of us can afford to miss even one practice."

"Yeah, I know," Kiki said. "But it can't be helped. We can't use the garage to practice anymore, either."

"What? Why?"

"The same reason Leo won't be joining us. He lost his job."

"He got fired?" Eligio's eyes bulged out.

"What happened?" Alvaro asked, as he took a bite of the cafeteria hamburger Cande handed him.

"His boss gave him a bunch of shit, and you know Leo," Kiki said.

"He didn't hit the guy, did he?" Eligio asked. "'Cause he could be arrested for that."

"Quiet, Elly," Alvaro told Eligio without taking his eyes off Kiki. "Where is he?"

"He went to his parents' place."

"He must really be wrecked," Alvaro said. "Why didn't he come to us?"

"When he called, he said he had to explain things to his family in person. You know; why he won't be able to send them money for a while."

"That's going to be tough. Especially with his brother depending on him. That technical school isn't cheap."

"One of us has to get out of this hole," Leo said as he plopped down next to Kiki. "Talking about me, girls?"

"Sorry about your job," Alvaro said.

"I'll get another one." Leo shrugged.

"I didn't think you'd be back this fast," Kiki said.

"No reason to hang around my folks' place feeling ashamed. And I made good time on the chopper."

"The garage let you keep it?" Alvaro asked.

"Screw them. I built it from parts; they just let me use their tools, and I figure I've paid them back with sweat. I'm just sorry we lost a place to practice."

"We can go back to my roof."

Leo shuddered. "No thanks."

"You're afraid of heights?" Eligio chuckled.

"So what?"

"Nothing. I just don't picture you being afraid of anything."

"I'm cautious," Leo said. "Leaping around near a long drop just isn't smart."

Kiki rolled his eyes. "Anyone have any ideas about where we could practice?"

Cande looked to Eligio. "What about the small auditorium?"

"I don't know," Eligio said. "I'd have to ask Mr. Matheson, and then I'd be responsible since I have a key to let the first year chorus in for before school practice."

"You have a key?" Kiki stroked his chin. "Interesting."

"No!" Eligio exclaimed, sorry he'd bragged about his privilege. "We're not going to sneak around."

"So you'll ask Mr. Matheson, right?" Alvaro said.

"Yes," Eligio said grudgingly. "But if any of you does anything to get me in trouble...." His voice trailed off. "Just don't do anything, okay?"

"Is it all right if we dance?" Leo asked, garnering a round of chuckles.

"You know what I mean," Eligio said.

"Don't worry so much. We won't betray your trust in us," Kiki said as the bell rang.

"I don't trust you." Eligio sighed as everyone got to their feet. "But I'll do whatever I can to help us win top prize."

"Good man," Alvaro said, slapping Eligio on the back. Eligio staggered forward and caught his balance just in time to receive a whack between the shoulder blades from Leo. Kiki laughed when Eligio flinched away as he passed by. As Eligio breathed a sigh of relief, Kiki reached up and smacked the back of Eligio's head… but not too hard. "Thanks, Elly," Kiki said as he hurried to catch up with Leo.

Eligio raised a hand to the back of his head as a smile spread slowly across his face. Picking up his book bag, he went to talk to Mr. Matheson.

"THIS is great," Alvaro said as he did a few steps on the auditorium's small stage. "And the sound is really good in here. Leo! Do you have that boom box plugged in yet?"

"Hang on. As soon as Elly's done whacking off in the outlet, we'll have music."

Eligio's outraged squawk carried clearly from the backstage area. "The extension cord is plugged in," he said sharply. "Don't turn it up too loud."

Kiki chuckled. "Eligio was born to fuss," he said, sliding down next to Cande to sit on the edge of the stage.

Cande stopped swinging his legs and glanced aside at Kiki, wary of the sudden overture. "If you say so. I don't know him well."

"Hey, Carlisle," Kiki said, leaning toward the other boy. "Don't be so standoffish. Maybe you're just shy, but you don't have to hold back around us. Especially when we're performing, you know? Try putting yourself out there a little more."

"What are my two favorite people talking about?" Alvaro asked, going to one knee behind Cande and resting his forearm on Kiki's shoulder.

"I was just telling Cande that he could smile a little more on stage."

"Yeah, that's good advice," Alvaro said. "The audience likes it if you look like you're enjoying what you're doing. That should be easy for us, right? Since we love what we do."

"Absolutely," Cande nodded, smiling up at Alvaro. He took the hand Alvaro offered and was hauled to his feet as if he weighed less than his shoes.

"Kiki?" Alvaro held out his other hand.

"Let's go," Leo called. "It'll be Eligio's bedtime soon."

Alvaro pulled Cande and Kiki into line and signaled Leo to start the music. Eligio ran over and got into place as Leo reached out and pushed "play." There was a moment of absolute stillness as the five young men waited for the song to start, and then they were in motion, stepping out together on the first note. They got halfway through before Cande made a misstep and threw the others off. He asked to see the step again, and Kiki whipped off a series of fluid moves. Cande nodded and Leo started the song over again. After three more renditions with various degrees of success, they took a break.

"Anyone have any song suggestions?" Alvaro asked as he unscrewed the cap of a plastic water bottle. "'Cause this one just sucks to me now. Why'd we pick it?"

"We only have nine days," Kiki said. "I agree that we need a better song, but if we're going to change it, we have to do it right fucking now."

"Maybe we should just stick with this one," Leo said. "It was a top ten song last summer, and besides, we already have our moves figured out.

"We still have to learn to sing it in harmony," Cande said.

"I thought you could sing lead, and we'd back you up," Eligio said.

Cande shook his head. "No way. We dance together and we sing together."

"Whoever sings it, we still need a song," Kiki said. "'Cause I agree with Alvaro; I'm just sick of this one."

"I have one," Eligio said.

"Well, what is it?" Leo asked.

"Promise you won't laugh?" Eligio said.

"Only if it's not funny," Kiki drawled.

"Well, I just thought of a song that we can find an instrumental track of, and it won't be too hard to lean."

"Just say it." Alvaro poked Eligio in the side.

"'Lucky Star' by Madonna."

"Madonna!" Kiki immediately went prone on the stage and did a raunchy impression of Madonna performing "Like a Virgin." Leo joined him, running his hands over Kiki's heaving, undulating body.

"I knew those two would make fun of me," Eligio said.

Cande turned from watching Leo and Kiki, wiping the smile from his face. "I think it's a good suggestion, and we don't have to sing it the way she did."

"The lyrics are kind of… simple, aren't they?" Kiki asked as he got to his feet, dusting off his clothes..

"That makes them easy to learn," Alvaro said.

"It'll sound amazing with a five part harmony on the chorus," Eligio said eagerly.

"Yeah, it will," Cande said slowly. "Each of us could have a couple of lines to sing solo on the verses, and then we hit the chorus hard with all five voices."

Eligio nodded eagerly. "I'll get started on an arrangement tonight. I really think the symbolism of a lucky star will bring us good—"

"Stay right where you are." A familiar male voice interrupted Eligio. The five young men stared up the aisle as Mr. Cruz walked into the light. "What are you punks doing here?"

"We have permission," Kiki said when it became obvious that Eligio was paralyzed with mortification.

"Who gave you permission?" Mr. Cruz challenged.

"Mr. Matheson said we could use the auditorium," Eligio said when Leo nudged him. "You can call him and ask."

"I've already called Mr. Matheson and left a message on his answering machine. He should be here soon, and he can decide if he wants the police to be involved."

"We aren't doing anything wrong," Alvaro said.

"You'll have to forgive me if I find it hard to believe you. I can see Leo Lazaro there, who has a record, and Candelario Carlisle, who shouldn't even be at this school. They should both be in jail. Why are you smirking, Enrique Viera? You might have more money, but you're just as bad as these others." He stopped in front of the stage. "Except perhaps for Eligio Domingo, but seeing him here with you punks doesn't give me much confidence in him."

"It doesn't sound like you have any confidence in any of us," Alvaro said.

"In my opinion, not one of you has an ounce of ambition to better yourselves. You're content to run around all night and sleep in school the next day. All you care about is getting high, getting laid, and getting out of work."

Kiki whistled, shocked to hear a teacher speaking with such brutal frankness. "Harsh."

"You think I'm harsh? Wait until you get out in the real world. You'll wish you'd paid a bit more attention in class."

"The real world?" Alvaro began when he felt Cande's hand on his arm reminding him how pointless it was to try to get an adult to listen.

"Yes, the real world, where you'll be expected to work for a living, to actually take responsibility for yourselves. Not one of you is ready for that," Mr. Cruz said.

"You don't know us." Everyone turned to look at Eligio, and the younger boy subsided, looking down at his feet.

"Are you sure you know your friends?" Mr. Cruz said. "Did you know that Leo Lazaro was arrested for dealing drugs? That Enrique Viera has a record of shoplifting? Or that Cande Carlisle should be in prison? I'm assuming you didn't know or you wouldn't be keeping company with them. People judge you by your friends, Eligio."

"That's true." Another man joined the conversation as he came down the central aisle. "Shall we talk about your friends, Mr. Cruz?"

"I don't think you should speak to me this way in front of students, Mr. Matheson."

"And I don't think you should speak to students in that belittling manner."

Mr. Matheson and Mr. Cruz locked eyes for a long moment before Mr. Cruz spoke again. "Perhaps I was a bit harsh."

"And ignorant." The music teacher's expression softened to a smile. "Ignorance is forgivable."

Mr. Cruz's eyes widened at this arrogance. He'd avoided interacting with the new music instructor on principle. Brooks Matheson was young, careless of his dignity, and showed a deplorable tendency to add colorful touches to his suits in the form of brightly patterned ties and vests. Mr. Cruz could see that he'd been wise to steer clear of this indecorous, snobbish oddball. "I don't need your forgiveness," he said.

"No, you need theirs." Mr. Matheson waved a hand at the five young men on the stage. "You owe them an apology."

Mr. Cruz's face curdled. "Why would I apologize to a bunch of delinquents?"

"Because you didn't bother to check your facts before condemning them. If I'm ever on trial, I'll pray that you aren't on the jury. If you'd waited for me to answer your phone message, you'd have known that these boys have my permission to be here, but I'm sure they told you that. Just as I'm sure you chose not to believe them."

"Why would I believe them?"

"You wouldn't, because you don't know them. You're judging them by things they did in the past. It's true that Leo was picked up with a large amount of marijuana, but he was only fifteen and he paid for the crime with community service. Anyone can make a mistake when they're young and inexperienced. Since he made his mistake, he's changed his life. He attends school regularly and then works a full shift at his job so he can send money to his family."

"I didn't know that," Mr. Cruz said. He cleared his throat. "That's very admirable."

"And isn't it just possible that there are things you don't know about each of these boys?"

"I suppose."

Mr. Matheson pushed his glasses up the bridge of his nose. "If I know these things about them, why don't you? Aren't they your students as well?"

Mr. Cruz cleared his throat again. "I thought I was doing you a favor by calling you. The next time I see something suspicious, I'll just ignore it and assume everything is fine."

Mr. Matheson pursed his lips, seeing that he was getting nowhere. "Thank you for calling me, Mr. Cruz. I can handle matters from here."

Mr. Cruz gave the other teacher a curt nod. "I was only doing my duty as an employee of this school."

"And not one iota more," Mr. Matheson murmured as Mr. Cruz turned to go.

Mr. Cruz's posture stiffened. "Be self-righteous while you can; you'll burn out soon enough." He stalked up the aisle and disappeared from view.

"Thank you, Mr. Matheson." Eligio's paralysis broke and he came forward. "Mr. Cruz threatened to call the police."

"I'm sure he did. How are the rehearsals going?"

"Well, we finally chose a song," Kiki said drolly.

Mr. Matheson smiled, the stage lights glinting on his white teeth and the lenses of his glasses. The smile broadened when he heard the title of the song. "You're not performing in the same costume Madonna wore, are you?" he chuckled.

"Of course not!" Eligio exclaimed.

"I don't know," Kiki said. "Maybe we should think about it. It sure would get attention."

"Yeah. The wrong kind," Eligio said. "We don't want people laughing at us."

"We should give it a shot." Leo wound Eligio up another notch. "It would be totally unique."

"For sure," Kiki enthused. "No one else will be wearing women's clothes." He paused. "Except for the women, of course."

Mr. Matheson chuckled again. "It's all right, Mr. Domingo. Your friends are just teasing you."

"It's not funny," Eligio said. "You don't know these guys. They'd do it. They'd put on dresses just to mess with me."

Kiki turned to Leo. "He's right."

"We would." Leo nodded.

"I don't think the Spring Festival Music Competition is ready for that," Mr. Matheson said.

"Thank you again for filling out the forms for us," Alvaro said.

"And for giving us a ride to the show," Eligio added.

"Yeah, none of us has a car, and we won't all fit on Elly's bike," Kiki said.

"I'm happy to help, and I really hope you'll do well. Now, it's getting a bit late; are you finished here? Does anyone need a ride home? No? I'm going, then. Thank you for locking up."

"I wish all teachers were like him," Eligio said as Mr. Matheson walked away.

"At this school?" Leo was skeptical. "They wouldn't last long. The nice ones never do."

"Mr. Matheson's been here almost two years," Alvaro said. "And now that he's adopted Elly, he'll have to stay for two more."

Eligio huffed, but was secretly pleased that Alvaro had given him a nickname, any nickname. "He said he'd help me with the arrangement and get a copy of the recording to play at the festival."

"That's cool," Leo said. "So are you guys going straight home?"

"I was," Alvaro said, glancing at Cande.

"I have to be in by nine," Cande said.

Kiki shrugged. "No plans."

"My folks are expecting me," Eligio said. "In fact, I should go. Mama likes us to all be at the table when she serves dinner."

"You're a lucky guy," Leo said, completely confusing Eligio.

"Whatever," Eligio said. "Come on, you guys. I have to lock up." He locked the side door, put the key in his watch pocket, and rode away on the rickety bike.

"You'd think his parents could afford a new bike," Leo said. "They own a grocery store after all."

"Big family," Alvaro said. "I'm taking off too. See you guys tomorrow." He put his arm around Cande's shoulders. "Walk with me for a ways?" he asked.

Cande ducked his head, but looked up at Alvaro from the corner of his eye. He could almost feel the aura of arousal emanating from Alvaro and expected to feel a static charge every time they touched. He knew better than to play with this kind of fire, but he was caught in a field of attraction too strong to resist. When Alvaro touched him, he forgot everything. All he wanted was for Alvaro to touch him again, to go on touching him as this amazing feeling grew with each caress. Cande had fooled around before—with girls and boys, men and women—but no one had ever made him feel like this. He'd never felt this eagerness, this anticipation, this yearning to be alone with someone just so they could hold each other. When Alvaro looked at him the way he was looking right now, Cande couldn't wait to be alone with him. He'd never intended for this to happen, but he wanted this boy in a way that made him ache. He was being very foolish, and he knew he'd pay for it, but right now—if Alvaro asked him to—he'd free-climb a skyscraper, wrestle a shark, anything to feel that glow of being wanted.

"Go on," Kiki said, giving Alvaro a push. "The tension is killing me."

"Yeah, go get a room," Leo said as Alvaro and Cande walked away. "Speaking of which," he said, glancing at Kiki. "I need a place to stay."

"No you don't. You're staying with me." Kiki put an arm around Leo's waist. "We'll work out a way for you to pay your rent."

"Fine, but I warn you, I don't do any kinky stuff."

Kiki grinned. "We'll have to work on that. Now let's pick up the pace. We don't want to miss the last bus to my side of town."

"Why would we ride the bus when we have my hog?"

"Your... *hog*?"

"Yeah, you know... my motorcycle."

"Oh right, your *hog*. I'm used to hearing chopper. Is it safe?"

"When did you turn into Elly? Come on. You can wear my helmet." Leo looked into Kiki's eyes. "Unless you're chicken, of course."

"Are you actually daring me? We're not at recess and more important, we're not in fourth grade."

Leo shrugged. "Are you riding with me or not?" He clucked for emphasis.

Kiki sighed and followed Leo to where the bike was parked. After unlocking the chain, Leo straddled the forked chopper and lifted it off the stand, muscles bunching in his bare arms. He took the helmet off the handlebars and tossed it to Kiki. Kiki put the helmet on and climbed on behind Leo. "Hold on," Leo said as he picked his feet up and twisted the throttle. Kiki hurriedly wrapped his arms around Leo's waist and held on as they sped down the street. He tightened his grip when the bike heeled over going around a corner and caught Leo's high-wattage grin in the side mirror. Determined not to show fear, no matter what Leo did, Kiki relaxed. In a few minutes, he was moving in concert with Leo, pressed against his muscular back, leaning with him in the turns. He could feel the wind flowing over him and the power of the engine between his legs, and the sensation was mixed up with the firmness of Leo's muscles under his hands and the smell of Leo's nape. When they pulled up at the curb of Kiki's apartment building, he was amused to find that he had half a hard-on. "I'm hanging around Alvaro and Cande too much," he muttered as he got off the motorcycle.

"What?" Leo put the bike on its stand and pulled off his gloves.

"Nothing."

"Will the chopper be safe here?"

"There's a parking lot attendant. Come on. I'm starving. Let's go see what's in the refrigerator."

"Your folks won't mind me being here?" Leo asked as they walked into the building.

"They're gone again." Kiki pushed the elevator button and looked up at the lighted numbers. "If any of the staff mention that I had a friend over, they'll probably be thrilled that I'm socializing. Don't worry about it."

"What if someone tells them you're hanging out with a delinquent on a bike?"

"My mother will probably ask for your phone number." Kiki looked over his shoulder as he opened the door to his apartment. "My dad might too."

Leo laughed as he followed Kiki into the foyer, and then Kiki flipped on the lights. "Sweet!" Leo said.

"You've been here before." Kiki shrugged, downplaying the wealth that embarrassed him. "It's not that special."

"Are you kidding? It's awesome." Leo stepped down into the sunken living room and did a slow spin, taking in the giant TV screen, the sound system, and the bar. "You're super-fly, man."

Kiki chuckled as he joined Leo. "That's me," he said, picking up the master remote and pointing it at the television.

"Seriously, I'll bet you've bagged plenty of babes up here."

"Are we being honest or are we being guys?"

"Okay, I'll stop slobbering on your apartment now," Leo said good-naturedly. "It really is cool, though. Thanks for inviting me."

"It's nice to have company. Since Cande Carlisle came along, we don't hang out like we used to. I mean, we hang out, sure, but it's all about the band now."

"Well, we're seniors now. We have more to think about than lifting six-packs from the corner shop or riding a skateboard all the way down the library railing."

"That doesn't sound like the Leo we all know and love and whose numerous casts we've signed."

"You started it by talking about Alvaro. Funny...." Leo's gaze flicked to the rapidly changing channels on the television. "I've known Alvaro since he moved here after his dad left. That was fifth grade, and even then I figured he'd get some girl pregnant and quit high school to work at the Walmart warehouse."

"Are you brooding about his alleged gayness again?"

"Well, it has kind of been on my mind."

"Does it really bother you?"

"It doesn't bother me that he's gay, or bi, or whatever, but it makes you think, doesn't it? I mean, dude, if a guy like Alvaro can be gay...."

"Anybody can?" Kiki finished for him. "I suspect you're right about that. Anyway, being gay doesn't mean dressing up like a showgirl."

"Fuck you," Leo said equably. "I'm not that ignorant."

"No? Well, are you thirsty? Hungry? I could eat a hippo."

"Sure." Leo followed Kiki into the large kitchen and watched him take stuff from the refrigerator and set it on the counter. "Is that pizza? I'll take a slice."

"I can put it in the microwave," Kiki said as Leo took a big bite. "Or not." He hopped up to sit on the faux-granite counter and took a long drink out of a juice bottle. "Help yourself to whatever you want."

"Can I have anything on the counter?" Leo leered.

"If you think you're man enough, come and get it, big boy." Kiki laughed as he spread his legs.

Leo moved closer, standing between Kiki's thighs as he looked up at him. "What are you going to do if I take you up on that?"

"I'm not worried." Kiki threw back another slug of orange juice.

Leo watched the muscles work in Kiki's throat as he replied. "Come on; admit it. You find me irresistibly sexy."

"Of course I do, but I know you'll never do anything."

"Maybe I've been thinking about it."

"Because of Alvaro and Cande?"

Leo nodded. "They're so... you know?"

"Yeah, I know. They practically glow."

"I want to feel like that."

"Who doesn't?" Kiki paused. "Are we still joking around?"

"Do you want to be joking around?

"I asked you first."

Leo took the plunge. "I really have been thinking about this. I've never really felt like *that* with a girl, so I thought maybe...."

"You thought maybe you'd try it with a guy?"

"Not just any guy."

"Are you saying you have feelings for me?"

Leo put his hands on the tops of Kiki's thighs and squeezed gently. "Would it be a problem if I did?"

Kiki's breathing became shallow as his heart rate increased. "No." His voice came out in a whisper, and he raised the juice to his dry mouth. He took a drink, and then Leo took the bottle from his hand, setting it on the counter. Grabbing Kiki's hips, Leo pulled him forward to the edge of the counter. "What are you going to do?" Kiki asked.

"Damned if I know, but I'm no chicken. Want to try kissing?"

"What the hell," Kiki murmured. Framing Leo's face between his hands, Kiki bent his head and touched his lips to Leo's before either one of them could think twice about it. In a split second, Leo knew that his long-held suspicions about why he hung out with guys and why sex with girls didn't ring his bell were true: he was gay. In the same tiny segment of time, all of Kiki's long-held fantasies about Alvaro were revealed for the unrealistic daydreams that they were; he didn't love Alvaro, at least not in that way. When the kiss ended, Leo and Kiki stared at one another for a very long time before Kiki broke the silence. "Well, that was enlightening."

Leo nodded. "How did we not realize this sooner?"

"You never offered me a ride on your hog before."

Leo grinned, relieved that Kiki was keeping it light. "I'm really not sure what to do. If you were a girl, I'd ask you to wrap your legs around me and I'd carry you out to the couch while I was kissing you. I'd lay you on the couch and kiss you some more while I tried to get your shirt off. Then I'd kiss you some more while I tried to get my hand down your pants. More kissing after you slapped me, and then I'd go home to toss off."

"Sounds good to me," Kiki said. "And the beautiful part is that you're already home."

"Yeah, but you're not a girl."

"Duh and so what?"

"Well, I don't know, but with a girl... they expect you to be all tender and romantic."

"You don't like tenderness and romance?"

"Yeah, I guess I do. I just wasn't sure if you did. You're so cynical."

"And you're so macho." Kiki ran his hand through Leo's short hair. "Let's try making out and see what happens," he said, wrapping his legs around Leo's waist.

"Oh man!" Leo gasped. "That's really turning me on."

Kiki chuckled, his voice dropping into a deeper register. "Why don't you take me over to the couch?" he said before he lowered his head to lick at Leo's pierced earlobe.

"Damn." Leo put his arms around Kiki and lifted him off the counter. Turning his head, he captured Kiki's lips, nibbling at them as he crossed the room. Kiki licked at Leo's full lips as Leo set him on the couch and pulled back. "Whoa, man! Give me a second."

"You're aren't getting cold feet, are you? I'm really interested in taking this further."

Leo smiled. "Me too. But do you think we should just jump right into having sex?"

"Who said we were having sex? We're necking."

Leo gave Kiki a dubious look. "Be honest."

"Okay." Kiki sighed. "I'm a big slut. I want to do everything with you, and I want to do it right now."

"Me too."

"But?"

"What if we're just excited because we're doing something kinky? What if we wake up in the morning and we can't look at each other?"

"Do you think that's going to happen?"

"No, but I don't want to take the chance."

"Leo?" Kiki gazed up at his friend, his expression somber.

"What?" Leo said apprehensively.

"You're so cool." Kiki put a hand on the back of Leo's neck and pulled him into a kiss. Leo settled on top of Kiki, running his hands down Kiki's sleek flanks and up under the hem of his shirt. Their tongues slid together as the kiss grew more passionate. Leo's fingers climbed the ladder of Kiki's ribs, and without warning he was tossed to the floor as Kiki exploded with laughter. "Ticklish," Kiki gasped as he rolled off the couch and threw a leg over Leo, leaning into him.

"I forgot how ticklish you are," Leo said. "I was going for your bra clasp." Kiki laughed as his mouth descended on Leo's in a kiss that surprised and delighted Leo all the way to his toes. "You're a good kisser," Leo said as Kiki let him up for air.

"Oh baby," Kiki drawled. "If you think that was good, you're in for a real treat." Grasping Leo's wrists, Kiki pinned his friend's hands to the carpet and took his mouth again. Leo relaxed and was amazed at how good it felt to give up control for a little while. Kiki's kiss stirred him to his core, and the way Kiki was moving his hips stirred everything else. Leo lifted his ass from the floor to increase the contact, and a bolt of sheer bliss tightened his groin, suffusing him with liquid heat. Pulling his hands free of Kiki's hold he grabbed Kiki's butt and pressed their crotches firmly together. "Oh yeah...." Leo felt Kiki's warm breath on his face, and then Kiki welded their mouths together again. Tongues entwined, hips pumping, and hearts pounding, they came in a mutual explosion of ecstasy and lay panting like marathon swimmers.

"Damn!" Leo breathed. "Damn...."

"Yeah. Damn."

"I can't move. I swear I can't move. I can barely breathe."

"Maybe because I'm on top of you?"

"No. I'm just blown away. That was the best ever."

Kiki blew out a big breath. "Yeah, for me too."

"It really pays to be brave sometimes."

"So you think this is a good thing?"

"It feels like a good thing." Leo folded his lips as he looked up into Kiki's jet black eyes. "What are you thinking?"

"I'm thinking that maybe we should keep this good thing to ourselves for a while."

"You mean not tell our parents? I wasn't going to anyway. They'd shit rainbow colors and die."

"Maybe our friends don't need to know either."

"Why can't Alvaro know? Are you ashamed of me?"

"Don't be a jackass. Of course, we can tell Alvaro, but Eligio—"

"Wouldn't understand," Leo finished for Kiki.

"So I'm just saying that we don't need to make an announcement or anything."

"Then I guess I better call the newspaper and cancel the article about our engagement."

Kiki shoved his thigh hard against Leo's crotch. "You're a funny guy when you loosen up." He paused. "But you don't appear to be going soft."

Leo groaned. "How could I go soft with you lying on top of me?"

"Interesting," Kiki said as he dipped his head to cover Leo's mouth with his.

"HERE we are," Alvaro said lamely as they reached the railroad tracks and stopped on the walkover. Cande rested his elbows on the guard rail and gazed into the distance. Alvaro leaned his back against the concrete and gazed at Cande's profile backlit by the streetlights. "What do you see out there in the dark?"

"I'm not looking at anything. I'm just feeling the night around me."

Alvaro slid closer until his hip touched Cande's. "I love you," he said.

"That makes the night even better."

"You're still such a Goth." Alvaro smiled as he reached out to stroke Cande's cheek. "Still wearing makeup." His eyes widened and he stroked Cande's face again. "What's this?"

Cande pulled away. "Nothing. I can't believe you're freaking out over a little makeup."

"Is that a bruise?"

"Yes. It's a bruise. Big deal."

"If it's no big deal, why did you hide it?"

"Because I knew you'd freak out."

Alvaro clenched his fists to contain the rage that erupted from his heart like a solar flare. "I'm not freaking out."

"Let me see your eyes." Cande forced Alvaro's chin up and looked into his eyes. A shiver ran through Cande's frame. "It isn't good to get that angry."

"You're acting like I'm some kind of homicidal maniac."

"I don't want to fight with you. You're just stirred up and looking for a way to work it off."

"How'd you get the bruise?"

"I got in a fight."

"With who?"

"I'm not going to tell you. It was my fight and it's over."

"What if it happens again? You should tell me who it was, and I'll make sure he never—"

Cande grabbed a handful of Alvaro's ragged black hair and pulled him into a kiss. Alvaro responded ardently, maintaining contact as he moved to stand behind Cande. Craning his neck, he kept possession of Cande's sweet mouth as his hands slid down Cande's abdomen to his crotch. Cande's breath caught as his boyfriend fondled him. He broke the kiss, his head tipping back as he gripped the railing with both hands. Alvaro molded his length to Cande's back, grinding his erection against the round buttocks. "You make me hard so fast," Alvaro whispered, his breath stirring the fine hairs on Cande's nape.

"This is a much better way to work off your aggression." Cande knew he'd said the wrong thing as soon as the words left his mouth.

"Is that what we're doing?" Alvaro asked.

"It was a joke. We're having fun. It's okay to joke, right?"

"Sometimes I just don't understand you, and this is one of those times."

"I say stupid things when I'm horny."

Alvaro caught Cande's hand and pulled it away from his crotch. "Are you doing this because you love me?"

"I'm doing it because you make my heart beat so hard and fast that I'm afraid my ribs will break." Cande put his free hand on Alvaro's chest. "I'm doing it because I feel like I have a fever whenever you look at me. I'm doing it because I want you more than I've ever wanted anything, including a family."

Alvaro put his hand over Cande's. "But will you always want me?"

"I don't know. How can I know that?"

"I know I'll always love you."

"How?"

"I just do."

Cande spun away from Alvaro. "I'm going to be late for curfew."

"Wait!" Alvaro caught up with Cande and grabbed him by the elbow. "I don't understand. What did I do?"

"There's nothing wrong. I'm just late. Let me go."

"You look mad."

"I'm not mad at you. Believe me. I could never be mad at you."

"Never?" Alvaro smiled. "How can you know that?"

Cande's lips curved upward despite his determination not to smile. "I just know."

"We know each other better than you think." Alvaro pulled Cande slowly toward him.

Cande raised his face for a kiss and then pulled away. "I really have to go."

"I'm sorry I acted all weird."

"Me too. I was looking forward to some serious action."

Alvaro cupped his crotch with an exaggerated expression of pain. "Don't remind me. I'm going to have to limp home."

Cande turned away with a smile. "You're not the only one."

As usual, Alvaro watched Cande walk away until he turned the corner. However, this time Alvaro ran after the other boy and peered around the corner. Moving stealthily, he followed his friend for several blocks through an increasingly rundown neighborhood. Cande opened a gate in a chain link fence and walked across a paved yard to a medium-sized one-story house. He pressed a buzzer beside the entry and the door opened. From across the street, Alvaro saw a man grab Cande by the front of his shirt and yank him inside. He now had the choice of letting Cande know he was spying on him or leaving Cande with someone who looked very short-tempered. After fifteen minutes of wavering, Alvaro turned and went home, knowing he was making the right decision and feeling like the world's biggest coward.

When he got to his apartment, his mother was mutely upset at being left alone for so long and refused to even look at her dinner or her son. Alvaro couldn't think of anything other than what might be happening to Cande, and he snapped at his mother to stop sulking. He barely slept and had vague nightmares of being run over by some large machine like a cross between a steamroller and a garbage truck. He woke up tired, made his mom's breakfast, and did his best to apologize. She stared silently at the television as the eggs turned to rubber, and eventually he gave up and left for school.

chapter **Five**

"HAVE you seen Cande this morning?" Alvaro asked as soon Leo and Kiki rode up.

Leo shook his head as he rocked the motorcycle onto its stand. Kiki watched Leo as he answered Alvaro. "We came straight from my place. Leo's going stay with me for a while until he finds somewhere to live."

"I asked him to meet me early," Alvaro said as though Kiki hadn't spoken.

"You know what a flake he is," Leo said and caught Kiki's frown. "What?"

"He's not a flake," Alvaro said.

"The hell he isn't," Leo said, still ignoring Kiki's signals. "It's cute, but kind of annoying."

"Hi, guys!" Eligio said as he skidded his bike to a stop. "What's going on?"

"Have you seen Cande this morning?" Alvaro asked.

"No, but it's not even seven-thirty yet."

"He was supposed to be here early."

Eligio shrugged. "He skips a lot. Mr. Matheson talked to him about it."

"What did Cande say?"

"It was a private conversation," Eligio said. "What's the big deal?"

"I think he's getting a rough time at home," Alvaro said.

"Then you should tell a teacher or a policeman," Eligio answered a bit primly.

"I think I'll just go over there and see what's going on. That's what I should've done last night."

"Bad idea," Kiki said. "If someone's beating on him, you'll end up in jail if you go over there. Why don't you try it Elly's way first?"

"Cande's got a bad bruise on his cheek. The kind you get when someone's fist hits your face."

"Is that why he was wearing makeup?" Leo asked. "I thought that was a little over the top for this school."

Alvaro nodded. "Who knows how many times he's had to cover up something like that."

"Then you should definitely tell an adult," Eligio said.

"What about Mr. Matheson?" Kiki said. "He likes Cande, right?"

"Good idea!" Eligio turned to Alvaro. "You should talk to Mr. Matheson. I'll go with you, if you want."

"Thanks," Alvaro said, putting a hand on Eligio's shoulder. "If Cande's not in Mr. Cruz's class, I'll go talk to Mr. Matheson."

MR. MATHESON took off his glasses and set them on his desk. "I'll speak quickly before the next class comes in. First, I hope you know how serious this is."

Alvaro nodded. "I know all you have is my word."

"That's true, but I meant the consequences of discovering that a child is being mistreated by a state guardian will be far-reaching and quite serious. It might be some time before you see the end of any action we decide to take."

"I just don't want Cande to be hurt anymore."

"Of course you don't. I'm glad you came to talk with me. I'll find out what I can about the people at the foster home. Please tell me that you'll wait to hear from me before you do anything about this yourself."

"I'll wait for proof," Alvaro said. "But if Cande shows up at lunchtime and looks like he's been worked over, I'll have all the proof I need."

"And then you'll come to me, and we'll call the authorities," Mr. Matheson said firmly.

Alvaro nodded. "Thanks for listening to me."

"Not all adults are like Mr. Cruz, Alvaro. And even he wasn't always such a Grinch."

Alvaro ran a hand through his hair as he stood. "I don't know. It seems like there aren't that many positive things in life, and my friends are all I've got. I'm not going to stand around and let something happen to one of them."

"Try not to worry too much. I'll bet Cande just decided to skip his morning classes."

"I hope so," Alvaro said, but he didn't really believe it. The rest of the day was a blur to him. He didn't notice the new dimension to Leo and Kiki's friendship. He didn't eat his lunch. He couldn't sit still to watch TV with his mom. By the time he met the other guys for practice he was ready to jump out of his skin.

"Boo," Cande said, moving out of the shadow of the stage curtains to wrap his arms around Alvaro from behind.

"Where were you today?" Alvaro spun in Cande's embrace to face him.

"I had things I needed to do."

"Why didn't you mention it last night?"

"I didn't know about it last night."

"You couldn't find a way to get a message to me?"

"I didn't know it was going to be such a big deal. Next time, I'll be sure and let you know my whereabouts." Cande looked up at Alvaro from under his lashes. "I missed you."

"I was worried about you."

"Why?"

"You have that bruise, and I thought someone where you're staying beat you up."

"I told you that was my business."

"If someone's hurting you, we need to make it stop."

"Varo, it means a lot to me that you care, but leave it alone, okay?"

"You can't expect me to stand by and see you get hurt. I can't do it."

"I'm not asking you to. You've got the wrong idea. Trust me."

"I'll trust you, if you promise to tell me if you're in trouble."

Cande leaned his forehead against Alvaro's and brushed his lips against the other young man's. "Yes, my hero," he murmured.

"What's going on back here?" Eligio said as he pulled the curtain aside. Seeing Alvaro and Cande with their arms around each other, he took a few steps backward. "I… I'm… I should be somewhere else," he stammered as he turned and hurried away.

"Damn," Alvaro said. "I was hoping I wouldn't have to have this particular conversation with Eligio for a while. He's just not going to understand."

"He doesn't know you like guys?"

Alvaro shook his head. "Hell no. He's very… traditional; his whole family goes to Mass together twice a week. He's probably in shock."

"Well, he really looks up to you and being gay doesn't exactly fit in with the whole macho Latino thing, not to mention the church."

"That's an understatement."

"You don't seem to sweat it much, though." Cande tilted his head and looked at Alvaro from a new angle. "You're not making out with guys in the cafeteria or anything, but you don't exactly try to hide it, either."

"If someone has a problem with the way I am, I'm happy to discuss it with them."

Cande smiled his slow smile. "Why do I get the feeling that you let your fists do the talking?"

Alvaro shook his head. "I let my feet do the talking. Kickboxer, remember?" He rapped his knuckles gently against Cande's forehead.

"You're being cute again. I've told you before that it isn't fair." Cande's face went sober in the middle of his teasing. "I'm sorry I caused trouble for you with Elly."

"You should have thought of that before you turned me queer."

Cande slapped Alvaro's cheek lightly. "Now you're just making fun of me, and I was sincere. I don't want to mess things up for you."

"Eligio had to find out sometime. He's just going to have to deal with it if we're going to stay friends."

"You'll explain it nicely, though, won't you?"

"Of course. Elly's like a little brother to me."

"I think you have a lot of little brothers, Alvaro Torres."

"What?"

Cande smiled and shook his head as he gave his boyfriend a shove. "Come on. Let's practice," he said, pushing Alvaro ahead of him onto the stage.

Eligio was visibly nervous for about half an hour before the rhythms of song and dance took over, and he was able put aside what he'd seen and concentrate. Cande was able to make it through the entire routine without missing a step, and everyone knew the lyrics and harmony parts by heart. They were far from smooth in integrating the two parts of their performance, but the goal was finally in sight. All it would take to create a flawless performance was hour after hour of rehearsal, repeating the words and actions until they were second nature, leaving no room for error. It would take dedication, intensity, and drive. Party of Five had all three. They also had abundant talent, shining good looks, and a camaraderie that was growing every day. The bond that was forming between them became part of their act; the closer they became, the better they performed together, and some of their little pranks and inside jokes became part of the act. When Mr. Matheson caught the end of a run-through five days before the festival, he was impressed.

"I can't believe how much progress you've made."

"Thank you, Mr. Matheson," Eligio said. "We're lucky that Alvaro, Leo, and Kiki turned out to have such amazing voices."

"Leo and Kiki have amazing voices," Alvaro corrected. "I sing a lot better than I thought I would, but I'm not amazing." He turned to look at Cande. "Cande is amazing, beyond amazing. The best singer I've ever heard."

"Candelario has a remarkable voice," Mr. Matheson agreed. "You're all very good, and I can see you've worked very hard. What sort of costumes will you wear?"

"We're still discussing that," Alvaro said. "Shirts and ties probably; we want to look… professional. We can't agree on whether we should match or not."

"Suits always look nice on young men," Mr. Matheson said. "You could all wear the same suit but each with one difference. One of you could have a red vest, for instance. If you're short of money, you could wear your school uniforms."

Alvaro's gaze went to Kiki. Kiki glanced around at his friends and tried to picture them as Mr. Matheson had described. He nodded to Alvaro. "It could work. At least, we could wear the jackets and shirts. Maybe with jeans. And like Mr. Matheson said, we could each wear something red like a shirt or a hat."

"I can't dance in jeans," Eligio said.

"Why blame the jeans?" Leo asked, leaning on Kiki's shoulder.

Kiki chuckled and then turned to Cande. "Cande, can you work with me for a few minutes? I want to trick my solo out a little more."

When Cande went to help Kiki hone his vocal solo, Mr. Matheson beckoned Alvaro down from the stage. Walking a short way down the aisle, they stopped at the fifth row, and the music teacher spoke quietly. "I found out what I could about the foster home. I don't have what the TV cop shows call *contacts*. I'm just a humble high school music teacher, but I was able to find out a few things from school board public records. It's a legitimate state-run home, but more of a halfway house than foster care. The young men living there are various ages. Cande's the youngest at eighteen and the oldest is twenty. Two are attending Summit Vocational over on Palmer Street. One has a job at an office supply store, and the other one is doing community service as a street cleaner. The place has only been in operation for about a year, and as far as I can tell, there haven't been any complaints."

"Are these guys criminals?"

"They've been in real trouble." Mr. Matheson glanced at the stage. "Which made me wonder why Cande was there. I was able to get some of his history, a little more than what's in his school record. He was given up for adoption at birth and went through a series of adoptions that didn't take. He has a record of absences and poor grades as well as anti-social behavior. None of it is too surprising, just rather depressing, except for one very serious incident. When he was sixteen, he was involved in a robbery with another boy his age, a Charles King. King was killed when he drew a weapon on police officers."

Alvaro looked over his shoulder at Cande before he spoke. "I can't believe he was involved in something like that."

"People get drawn into things, usually out of a misplaced sense of loyalty, especially young people." Mr. Matheson sighed. "I assume he's on some sort of probation, but I don't know what for. The robbery was almost three years ago, and Cande was a minor at the time."

"I'm having a hard time believing this. Cande's just not like that. He's no low-life criminal; he's smart and really nice."

"People do things for all sorts of reasons," Mr. Matheson said. "You know how easily a good person can fall into bad ways. Leo has a record, and you don't think of him as a low-life, do you?"

"You're right," Alvaro said. "I didn't think before I said that."

"Only Cande knows why he went along with an armed robbery. I'm afraid if you want to know what happened, you'll have to ask him."

"He must've had a good reason."

"I'm sure he thought he did. I like Cande. I don't think he means anyone any harm, and he has the most beautiful voice I've ever heard. I really want him to do well."

"So do I. Thank you for your help, sir."

"I'm afraid that unless Cande tells someone in authority that he's being mistreated, there's not a lot more we can do without me becoming directly involved."

Alvaro cocked his head to the side. "How?"

"I'm Cande's teacher; I could request a visit to his home."

"You'd do that?"

"I'd most likely lose his trust, but at least I could put both our minds to rest about a few things."

"Mr. Matheson!" Eligio called. "Would you listen to us sing and give us a critique? Alvaro, come on; get up here!"

Alvaro and Mr. Matheson turned to see the other four in a semi-circle on the stage. Kiki waved. "Come on. We've got my solo worked out. Let's run through it before we go."

"Let's talk again tomorrow," Alvaro said to Mr. Matheson before he vaulted onto the stage and took his place between Eligio and Cande. He bumped Cande's shoulder and smiled when Cande looked up at him. "Count us in," he said.

Cande returned Alvaro's smile, took a deep breath and counted one, two, three and four, hitting the opening note of the song and holding it until the others found their harmony. He sang the first line. Leo and Kiki joined him on the second line, and Eligio and Alvaro came in on the third in a complex layering of sound that blended into one perfect tone. They didn't try dancing to the song; they just concentrated on singing it as perfectly as they could. Mr. Matheson stood without moving until the last note died away.

"That was wonderful, absolutely wonderful. I'm very impressed, gentlemen."

All five young men bowed and thanked the music teacher.

"Are you going to sing it that way at the competition? Without music?"

"We haven't talked about it," Eligio said.

"You should consider it. Your voices don't need accompaniment."

"Won't we look goofy dancing without music?" Leo asked.

"Your voices *are* music." Mr. Matheson picked up his jacket off the seat next to him. "You're good, really good. I look forward to watching you win the competition."

"Mr. Matheson really thinks we have a chance," Eligio said as he finished locking up and joined his friends on the sidewalk.

"We all heard him," Leo said.

"Yeah, that's really cool," Kiki said on a yawn. "I'm really tired. See you guys tomorrow."

"Yeah, see you tomorrow," Leo said as he walked away with Kiki.

"What's their hurry?" Eligio asked as Kiki climbed on the back of Leo's motorcycle.

"Yeah," Cande said, watching Kiki wrap his arms around Leo's trim middle. "What's their hurry?"

Out of Eligio's line of sight, Alvaro bumped his crotch against Cande's hip. "I'm kind of in a hurry too," he said.

"Me too," Eligio said, climbing on his bike. "We're having pork roast for dinner. See you tomorrow."

"Bye, Elly," Alvaro called after him.

Cande fell into step with Alvaro as they crossed the deserted nighttime campus keeping to the shadow of the building. Alvaro hung his arm casually across Cande's shoulders, inclining his head to look into Cande's face. "You trust me, don't you?" he asked.

Cande stopped just beyond the circle of light cast by a street lamp. "Whatever you're going to say will have to wait. I need to be in early tonight."

"You didn't mention it before."

"I'm sorry, but I really have to go. I'll see you tomorrow, okay?"

"Okay? No, not really. I was planning on spending a few minutes of quality time with you."

"It hurts me as much as it hurts you," Cande said. "I wouldn't leave you if I didn't have to."

Alvaro pulled Cande into his arms and kissed him. "See you tomorrow," he said as he let go.

"Thanks for understanding."

"I'm doing my best."

Cande sighed. "You're too good for me. Say hi to your mom, okay?"

"Of course." Alvaro kept his hands in his pockets as Cande looked left and right and then stretched to kiss him on the lips. "Be safe."

"Thanks." Cande shouldered his backpack and walked away.

Alvaro waited for him to turn the corner before he followed.

chapter Six

ALVARO cursed under his breath, and his suspicions grew when Cande took a different route. Keeping out of sight, he followed the other young man to a market district and watched him walk up to a parked car. The driver's door opened, and a thirtyish guy in a suit got out. He joined Cande, and they strolled away between the carts and stalls of the street market. Alvaro's heart crumpled with a sharp, savage pain when the stranger put his arm familiarly around Cande's shoulders. Gritting his teeth, Alvaro followed them until he was within earshot.

"Why don't you believe me?" Cande was saying.

"Because you're a liar," the man in the suit said.

"I'm not lying to you."

"And I suppose you don't know that your little playmate is hiding in the Dumpsters behind us."

Cande spun around, staring into the mouth of the alley, and Alvaro froze. "What are you talking about?" Cande said.

"That pretty-boy thug you've been leading around by the dick. I spotted him when I got out of the car. You must really have a hook in him." The man shook his head. "I told you to make friends, not conquests."

"Varo?" Cande called uncertainly.

"Come on out, kid," the man said. "No point in hiding anymore."

Feeling a little foolish, but bolstered by his concern for Cande, Alvaro stood and walked out of the alley. Nervousness and pride made him square his shoulders and put a swagger of attitude in his stride.

Cande groaned. "Ah, shit! I knew you gave in too easily when I said I had to leave. Why did you follow me?"

"Who's this?" Alvaro asked, pointing at the stranger.

"I don't have time for adolescent jealousy." The man ignored Alvaro and spoke to Cande. "I'm leaving. This has been a complete waste of my evening. I hope it doesn't become a pattern."

"I can't make things happen faster," Cande said.

"Now that's just not true. You know how to make things happen. And if you're smart, you'll get me what I need soon."

Alvaro heard the implied threat and took a step toward the other man. "Alvaro, don't!" Cande said. "Just give me a minute, and then I'll explain, okay?" Alvaro stayed where he was, but his eyes never left the man who'd threatened Cande.

"Mr. Lopez," Cande said softly, "don't you think I want this to be over?"

Lopez sighed. "I really want this, Carlisle." He flicked a glance at Alvaro over Cande's shoulder. "Call me tomorrow and tell me something good." Without another word, he turned and stalked away.

"Who was that asshole?" Alvaro growled.

Cande took his boyfriend's arm. "Let's go get some ice cream."

"What?"

"We have a lot to talk about, and ice cream always makes me feel better."

"Are you going to tell me who that guy was?"

"I don't like your tone. Considering you were spying on me, you might want to dial the 'tude back a few notches."

Alvaro grabbed Cande by the upper arms and shoved him against the side of the building. "What the hell is going on? Was that the guy that's hurting you? Why did you lie to me and come here to meet him?"

Cande stared into Alvaro's eyes until the other young man let go of him. "Don't ever do that again unless we're fooling around and I ask you to play rough," he said.

"Is there fooling around in our future?"

"Why wouldn't there be?"

"I don't know. Maybe we should ask the guy whose name I don't know that you're sneaking around to see."

"I'm confused. Are you afraid for me, or are you jealous?"

Alvaro took a deep breath through his nose. "Both… I think. I'm pretty confused myself."

"Come on." Cande took Alvaro's arm and pulled him out of the alley and down the street. "Wait here," he said as he ducked into a store. He came back with two ice cream bars and handed one to Alvaro. "Come on. I'm screwed for curfew anyway. Let's walk to the park."

Alvaro unwrapped his ice cream and took a bite. "Chocolate-covered strawberry?"

"I took a chance. If you don't like it, I'll trade you."

"What do you have?"

"Coconut tarantula crunch."

"That doesn't exist."

"It's just vanilla. Want to trade?"

Alvaro shook his head. "I just want to know what's going on."

"I shouldn't tell you. I'll get in so much trouble."

"Then don't tell me." Alvaro took another bite of the ice cream bar and threw the rest into a trash bin at the park entrance.

"I want to tell you."

"That's different." Alvaro took Cande's hand. "So who was that rude guy?"

"Pelayo Lopez. He's a cop."

Alvaro absorbed his surprise before he spoke. "So is he like your parole officer or something?"

Cande shook his head as he swallowed the last of his ice cream. "He's a detective. There've been reports of abuse in the rehab system, and I'm helping him get evidence."

"Why you?"

"Because I said I would." Cande walked over to the children's play area and sat down on a swing.

Alvaro sat sideways on the next swing over. "Why?" he repeated.

Cande lowered his eyes. "I'm paying for something." His tongue came out to moisten his lower lip. "I did something really stupid and I should be in jail, but I made a deal." He closed his eyes. "I was an accomplice to a robbery where someone was killed. But since I didn't participate in the actual crime, and I wasn't armed, my court-appointed lawyer was able to keep me out of prison by feeding me to the police as an informant. Then I got caught with a controlled substance, and they had an excuse to keep me a while longer. I just keep getting into trouble and having to dig myself out, but the hole keeps getting deeper." Cande paused again. "When I came to this school, I didn't intend to make friends, no matter what Lopez wanted. I sure as hell wasn't going to help him bust some kids for whatever just to pad his arrest record. I was going to do what I had to as quick as I could and move on when it was over. I didn't know I was going to meet you."

"That made a difference?"

"You know it did. Once I saw how nice it was to have someone who… who really cared about me…." Cande's voice trailed off.

"What?" Alvaro prompted. "You can't just leave it there."

"I don't want to leave."

"I won't let that happen," Alvaro said firmly. "How long do you have to work for this cop?"

"Until he arrests someone."

"There's really abuse going on?"

Cande nodded. "Yeah, there's abuse. I just don't know how to get evidence."

Alvaro's eyes narrowed. "What about your bruises? Aren't they proof enough?"

"Mr. Simenon, the supervisor in charge of my house, has a really heavy hand, but it would just be my word against his. I need someone else to testify that he's hit them, and so far, I haven't had any luck. I haven't even seen anyone else getting hit."

"So this Simenon guy is the one who hurt you. Where is he right now?"

Cande smiled. "My hero," he said. "I didn't tell you what I was doing when we became friends because at first, I thought you wouldn't believe me. I tried really hard to keep a distance from you, but I liked you too much. I hope you're not super mad at me."

"I'm not mad at you." Alvaro reached across to put his palm against Cande's cheek. "I'm mad that you're being used. I'm mad that you had to keep secrets from me. I'm really mad that some asshole hit you. *Aiy!* I want to kill him."

"Well you can't. If you kill him and get caught, you'll go to prison, and I'll really miss you."

Alvaro wrapped his hand around the plastic-coated chain of Cande's swing and pulled him closer. "You would?"

"Of course I would." Cande curled his fingers around Alvaro's hand. "With you behind bars, who'd rescue me?"

"I'd find a way," Alvaro said, looking into Cande's eyes. "If you needed me, I'd be there."

Cande bit his lip, his eyes sliding away from Alvaro's earnest gaze. "I haven't been completely honest with you."

"It doesn't matter what you say, I'll still love you."

"Falling in love too fast is not a good thing."

"You say that like falling in love is a choice."

"Maybe we can't choose who we fall in love with, but we don't have to go rushing blindly into it without thinking about the consequences."

"Cande, you're barely eighteen. Everyone makes mistakes when they're young. It's part of growing up."

"We're the same age," Cande pointed out. "So don't lecture me, okay?" The tension went out of him as abruptly as it had appeared. His shoulders slumped, and he looked at the ground as he continued. "Some mistakes last longer than others. Some are forever."

Alvaro stood and pulled Cande out of the swing, hugging him tightly. "What did you do that was so bad?"

"I broke my word. I let Chaz die alone."

"Who's Chaz?"

"Charley King. He loved me, and I promised him I'd stay with him forever, but I couldn't do it. I was scared. I didn't want to die."

"This Chaz guy made you promise you'd die with him?"

Cande nodded. "We made a pact when we decided to run away from the home we were in: we would live or die together, no matter what. We swore in blood." He leaned back so he could see Alvaro's face. "We were hiding at Chaz's cousin's house, but we needed money to leave town, you know? Chaz said the quickest way to get some was to rob a gas station. He said it wouldn't be like stealing from a person. It would be like taking money from the oil company. So we picked out a place and walked in, and Chaz told the guy to give us the money. I swear I didn't know he had a gun. I don't know if his cousin got it for him or if he stole it from his cousin. I don't even know if it was loaded. The guy must have hit some silent alarm, and the cops were there in seconds. One of them shot Chaz as soon as they saw the gun. I should have stood up and let them shoot me like I said I would, but I hid behind the counter until they came to take me away. I'm a coward, and I let him die alone."

"That's crazy talk. If bullets were flying, I'd hide too."

"My love just wasn't as strong as his."

"That guy didn't love you."

"Don't say that." Cande pulled away from Alvaro. "Chaz loved me."

"I believe you loved him, or you thought you did, doesn't matter which. But he couldn't have loved you if he wanted you to die. He should've wanted you to live and be happy."

"He wanted us to be together forever."

Alvaro shook his head. "That's not love; that's ownership, and there's no reason for you to feel bad about breaking a promise like that."

"I do feel bad, though."

Alvaro hugged Cande tighter. "I wish I could make it all go away. I wish you'd grown up here and we'd met in first grade. I wish—"

Cande stopped Alvaro's words with a kiss. Lacing his fingers behind the taller boy's neck, he drew him down as he sat on the swing again. Alvaro straddled Cande's lap, taking control of the kiss, excitement rising in him like bubbles in champagne, clearing away the darkness raised by Cande's words. Cande clutched at the chains that held the swing up as the force of Alvaro's passion pressed him backward. Alvaro put a supportive arm around Cande's back, but didn't break contact with his mouth. Kissing Cande was like stepping into a wind tunnel of heated air that enveloped him like billowing silk and tore away all reason, logic, and coherent thought. Alvaro was aware of nothing beyond the sweet, wet heat of Cande's mouth, the soft smoothness of Cande's skin, and the citrus-ginger smell of Cande's shampoo. He wanted to dwell in this moment forever, and at the same time, he wanted to rush headlong to the blissful finale. With trembling fingers, he caressed the peach-skinned curve of Cande's cheek, the elegant line of his neck and the delicate collar bones. Breaking the kiss, his lips traced the path of his hand until the position became too awkward to continue as he wished. Cande made a small needy sound, and he reached blindly up as Alvaro's weight lifted from his thighs. Alvaro looked down at Cande's misty eyes, the softly parted rosy lips, and felt an upsurge of lust coupled with such an intense desire to protect this boy that it nearly put him on his knees. "Come here," he said, his voice thick with emotion, as he took Cande's hand and pulled him to his feet.

Cande wrapped his arms around Alvaro and gazed trustingly up at him. "Whatever you want," he murmured.

Alvaro swallowed hard. He thought of himself as fairly experienced for his age; he'd been with at least a dozen girls and boys and had even gone all the way with a couple of the girls, but at this moment, he felt exactly the way he had just before his first kiss. Whatever happened next would be unlike anything he'd ever done, because he was going to do it with Cande. Vibrating with excitement, nervousness, and elation, he did his best to speak in a normal voice. "You said you couldn't go home; do you want to stay at my house tonight?"

Cande nodded. "Yeah, let's go."

Alvaro let go of Cande only to slip an arm around his waist as they started walking. "I want you to be mine," he said after a brief silence."

"Aren't we already boyfriends?"

"Yeah, but I want it to be more than that."

"I'll sleep with you," Cande said instantly.

Alvaro had to catch his breath before he replied. "You almost gave me a heart attack."

"It's what you want, isn't it?"

Alvaro stopped and faced Cande. "Yeah, I want you. I want you so much that I feel like I'm going to explode into a million pieces when you touch me, but I don't want you to do it because you feel like you have to."

Cande stared at the ground between Alvaro's sneakers for a long time before he spoke again. "You must think I'm a total slut."

"No! Hell no!" Alvaro took Cande by the upper arms. "You're the opposite of a slut."

"So I'm a prude?"

Alvaro didn't know how to answer until he saw Cande's smile. "Yeah, that's right. You're a big prude. I don't know why I stay with you."

Cande chuckled. "Because you know I'll give in to your awesome sexiness eventually."

"Never doubted it." Alvaro smiled. "But it's important to me that you know you don't have to buy my love, not with money, not with sex, not with anything. I want to be your lover, but even if we never slept together, I'd still want to be part of your life."

Cande didn't say anything, but he put his arm around Alvaro as they finished the walk home. His guilt over Chaz hadn't been magically lifted away, but it was a lot lighter. He'd confessed his worst crime, and Alvaro hadn't turned away from him. Cande was going to find a way to show his self-appointed champion how grateful he was.

"IT'S not a very big bed," Alvaro said as he showed Cande into his room. "Maybe you'd like to sleep on the couch."

Cande shook his head. "I don't care if we don't do anything, but I want to sleep next to you."

"Okay." Alvaro took Cande's backpack from his shoulder and set it on the floor. "You might have to sleep on top of me, though."

"It's my favorite position," Cande joked.

"If you keep saying things like that...." Alvaro let the sentence hang.

"What?" Cande challenged with an impish smile. "What will happen?"

"Keep pushing me and you'll find out."

Cande put his hands on Alvaro's chest and shoved. Alvaro took a half-step back and caught himself. Giving Cande a stern look, he shook a finger at him. Cande laughed and Alvaro swept him into his arms. "As penalties go, this doesn't seem so bad," Cande purred.

"I want everything to be good for you from now on."

"Why? Why do you care so much about someone like me?"

"Someone like you? I'm not sure what that means. To me, you're only the most beautiful, wonderful, kind and caring person in—"

Cande put his fingers on Alvaro's lips. "Okay. Enough. If that's how you see me, I'd be stupid to try and change your mind." Moving his hand, he gave Alvaro a gentle kiss before he stepped away from him.

"Do you want to take a shower or something?" Alvaro asked to cover his disappointment when Cande left his arms.

Cande shook his head as he shrugged out of his jacket and began unbuttoning his shirt. Alvaro's tongue came out to swipe at his lower lip as Cande let the shirt fall to the floor. Cande toed off his shoes, unzipped his trousers, and stepped out of them. Clad only in white socks and briefs, he looked shyly up at Alvaro.

"Wow," Alvaro breathed. "You're beautiful all over." Drawn like iron to a lodestone, he moved closer to Cande, putting his hands on the other boy's hips. Softly, he brushed his lips over Cande's as he hooked his thumbs in the elastic waistband of Cande's underwear. He felt Cande's sharp intake of breath as he slid the briefs down over the curve of Cande's ass. The soft cotton hung up for a second on Cande's hardening cock and then pulled free. Cande's arousal bobbed back up as Alvaro sank to his knees, dragging the underwear down Cande's long legs. Cande lifted one foot and the other, and then Alvaro dropped the unwanted undergarment to the floor. "I feel like I might pass out," Alvaro said as he looked up.

Cande smiled and put a hand on Alvaro's glossy black hair. Stroking the thick silk, he pulled Alvaro's head forward. Alvaro didn't need any more encouragement. Wrapping his arms around Cande's thighs, he buried his face in Cande's crotch. Cande moaned as Alvaro nuzzled at his growing length, soft lips grazing the shaft, coaxing it to aching tautness. "That feels amazing," Cande said, running his fingers through Alvaro's hair. He wanted to ask Alvaro to stop, to suggest that they make out for a while first, but the feel of Alvaro's mouth on him stole his ability to express anything but pleasure. "So good," he whispered as Alvaro licked at the head of his cock.

"You taste like the ocean," Alvaro said, lips moving against sensitive skin.

"I hope you like the ocean."

Alvaro rose, sliding the length of Cande's body until they were face to face. "I haven't been to the ocean in almost a year. I used to spend most of every day there."

Cande put his hands on Alvaro's shoulders. "I didn't mean to make you sad."

"You didn't." Alvaro turned his head to kiss Cande's fingers. "You make me happy."

"Why don't you make *me* happy and take your clothes off?"

Alvaro grinned. "Can't wait to get a look at this magnificent body, can you?"

"Let's see what I've been missing."

Alvaro let his eyes travel slowly from Cande's face to his feet and back. "I hope you'll be as pleased as I am."

Cande smiled and held his arms out from his sides. "You like what you see?"

"You're gorgeous," Alvaro said again. "I've never seen anything as beautiful as you."

"You sure I'm not too skinny?"

"You'll fill out."

Cande smacked Alvaro hard on the chest. "So you *do* think I'm too skinny."

"I think you're perfect," Alvaro said quickly as he whipped off his T-shirt and threw it over his shoulder. He put his hands on Cande's slim waist and kissed him. "You'll always be perfect to me," he said as he kissed his way to Cande's left ear. Cande gasped as Alvaro nipped his earlobe, running his tongue over the silver stud earring. Alvaro slid his hands down to Cande's butt and pulled him closer. Cande gave a low moan as his arousal rubbed against the front of Alvaro's jeans, against suede-soft denim and the coolness of a metal chain.

"Take them off," Cande said breathlessly. "I want to see you."

Alvaro reluctantly let go of Cande—his mouth watering for another kiss—and rapidly shed his shoes and trousers. Cande barely got a glimpse before Alvaro embraced him again, diving on his lips. Cande's soft whimper escaped into Alvaro's mouth as their cocks touched skin to skin for the first time.

"Wait!" Cande gasped as he broke the kiss. Putting his hands on Alvaro's smooth chest, he pushed away from him. "Let me see."

With touching hesitation, Alvaro stepped back and spread his arms the way Cande had done. "What you see is what you get," he said, trying for a light tone and failing completely.

"How did I get so lucky?" Cande said. "You have the body of a god."

Alvaro blinked. "I do?"

"As if you didn't know! Just look at you. Look at your shoulders, your chest, those abs! I want to lick every inch of you."

"I have no objections. Which inches would you like to taste first?"

"I'm going to start right here," Cande said, putting a forefinger on the notch between Alvaro's collar bones. Dipping his head, he ran his tongue around the V-shaped depression.

Alvaro groaned as Cande's tongue ran up the line of his throat. "I'm so turned on; if you touched my dick right now I'd go off like a moon rocket."

Cande's soft laugh tickled Alvaro's ear. "Are you talking about this?" His knuckles grazed Alvaro's hardness, and Alvaro sucked in a big breath. "Are you sure it's a dick? Looks more like a boa constrictor to me."

Alvaro dropped his head, his cheeks going pink. "It's not that big."

Cande boldly wrapped his fingers around the long shaft and squeezed. "It's the biggest I've ever seen in person."

"I hope that's okay."

"Okay?" Cande's laugh pealed out. "Only you would say something like that. Any other guy would be strutting."

"It's not like I built it myself. It just grew that way."

Cande laughed again and clapped a hand over his mouth. "Oh shit! What about your mom?"

"Can you hear the TV?"

"Yeah."

"Then she can't hear us. Don't worry about it. It's not like she's going to get up and come in here. Hey!"

Cande gave Alvaro a look of unlikely innocence as he ran the ball of his thumb around the head of Alvaro's cock again. "What? You don't like it?"

"You're going to make me come if you keep doing that."

"I want to make you come."

"Let's kiss some more first."

"You really are different. Most guys go straight to the hand job."

Alvaro clamped down on the sudden flare up of jealousy and refrained from asking how many guys had enjoyed Cande's favors. He told himself that it didn't matter. He wasn't exactly a virgin himself. What came before was the past, and he was Cande's future. "I like making out," he said. "Hope that's not too weird."

"Me too. I'm really glad we both feel the same way." Cande slid his fist up the resilient flesh in his hand. "You have a beautiful cock, by the way."

"He thinks you're pretty too."

"He?" Cande chuckled. "Does he have a name?"

"You can call him 'Yours'."

Cande dropped his head, and his hand went still on Alvaro's arousal. After a moment, he looked up again, his eyes sparkling with tears. "It's too much," he said in a hoarse whisper. "I don't deserve anything this good."

"Shut up," Alvaro said. "I don't care what you think you deserve. You're mine and I'm going to take care of you, and there's not a damned thing you can do about it. Understand?"

Alvaro's words surprised a laugh out of Cande even as the tears spilled over to run down his cheeks. "I have no choice, then?"

"None. We belong together and that's that."

"Okay. Just this once, I'll let you tell me what to do."

Alvaro licked at the wetness on Cande's face until he got to his mouth. Cande met him eagerly, lips moving against Alvaro's, tongue darting into Alvaro's mouth in a groin-tingling caress. In moments, the only sounds in the room were moans and gasps as desire slipped the leash. Fingers, lips, tongues, teeth, and several other body parts were put to use in discovering pleasure zones and exploiting them energetically, enthusiastically, greedily. With less than gentle pressure, Alvaro bore Cande to his back on the narrow bed. Eagerly, Cande gathered Alvaro in, wrapping him up with arms and legs, cradling him fiercely. Welded at the mouth and groin, they moved against one another, skin sliding on skin in the first steps of the oldest dance. Alvaro moved to the music of Cande's sighs and whimpers, kissing, stroking, sucking, and nibbling as he pulsed his hips to the tempo that drew the loudest sounds from his lover. Cande locked his legs around Alvaro's thighs, pressed his feet against the insides of Alvaro's knees, and lifted his butt from the mattress. Alvaro groaned at the increased friction as Cande's cock slid the length of his before rolling to the side. "Fuck! I'm gonna come any second," he said breathlessly, as he thrust in counterpoint.

"Varo!" Cande gasped, biting his lower lip to hold in a cry as his whole being clenched in a strong spasm that released with a burst of pleasure, flooding every cell.

Alvaro slowed his stroke, watching as pale rose tinted Cande's creamy skin. He waited for Cande to open his eyes, looking down into a gaze as full of stars as the Milky Way. Barely moving his hips, he eased his hard length along the shaft of Cande's spurting cock. Cande groaned and clutched at Alvaro's ass, fingertips sinking into solid muscle. Alvaro continued to grind languidly against Cande, angling his head to take Cande's mouth in a slow, sweet kiss as his cock glided through the slick of Cande's cum. Cande responded ardently, pressing against Alvaro as though he meant to absorb him, relinquishing his lips only to kiss everything else he could reach.

"Varo," Cande sighed, his lips moving against Alvaro's ear. "You make me feel so good."

Alvaro dropped his head, biting into Cande's shoulder as he came in a racking shudder that ran the length of his frame. He held tight to Cande's hips as his seed squirted out between them. Cande held Alvaro close as they lay unmoving with their joy still reverberating through them. The house was quiet around them, and street noises were few at this hour. For a few minutes, they could pretend they were alone on their own little island and had no responsibilities to the outside world.

"Did that feel as good to you as it did to me?" Cande asked softly.

"You mean was it the best I've ever had? Times infinity?"

"Yeah. That good."

Alvaro nodded, a smile curving his lips. "It was… transcendent. I knew I was in trouble as soon as I saw you, Candelario Carlisle."

"In trouble?"

"*Aiy*, bad choice of words." Alvaro nuzzled at Cande's neck. "But I was interested in you as soon as you walked into class."

Cande chuckled. "I noticed you too."

Alvaro shifted, moving to lie against Cande's back and pulling him close. "Mama told me that she fell in love with my dad at first sight. I always thought she was just being a silly woman, but the first time I saw you, I knew."

"What did you know?" Cande had never believed in things like love at first sight, but he loved the feel of Alvaro's arms around him, Alvaro's breath on his nape, Alvaro's reviving arousal pressed to his butt. Cande felt warm, safe, and wanted. He'd listen to any sort of nonsense if he could just stay here forever.

"I knew you were mine." Alvaro tightened his arms around Cande. "I knew I'd do anything for you."

"How did you know I'd feel the same?"

"I didn't."

"You have a lot of faith."

Alvaro chuckled, and the sound traveled from Cande's ears directly to his groin. Cande's cock stirred, and he reached down to adjust his position.

"Are you comfortable?" Alvaro asked instantly. "It's really a small bed, I know."

"I'm fine." Cande took one of Alvaro's hands and moved it down.

Alvaro was quick to take the hint. "What's this? Hard again already?"

"And what's that poking me in the ass?"

Alvaro pushed his knee between Cande's legs, parting them as he took hold of Cande's stiffening shaft. "It's your new best friend saying hi," he said, making Cande giggle.

"More like Godzilla heading for Tokyo." Cande laughed again.

Alvaro kissed Cande's shoulder. "I'm not going to do anything you don't want. You don't ever have to be afraid of me."

"Do I sound scared?"

"No, you sound like the smartass that you are." Alvaro pressed forward, rubbing his cock up and down the cleft of Cande's backside.

Cande pushed back, increasing the contact, making Alvaro moan. "You like that, huh?"

"I could stand it for a while." Alvaro squeezed Cande's arousal. "But after four or five days, I'd probably get tired."

"Hang on a second." Cande reached between his legs, until he could get his fingers around Alvaro's dick. Bending the shaft down,

Cande pulled it between his thighs. "Wish we had some lotion or something," he said as he clamped his legs together.

"I don't want to let go of you long enough to get up and get some."

"Have you done this before?"

Alvaro nodded, unable to speak as Cande toyed with the head of his cock. It occurred to him that he still had Cande's hard length in his hand, and he began to stroke it slowly.

Cande spat into his free hand and rubbed the saliva onto Alvaro's dick. "You're wet already," he said with a trace of smugness.

"You could make me come just by looking at me." Alvaro groaned as Cande tugged on his shaft. "I've never wanted anyone like this."

"Me, either," Cande confessed. "Why don't you let Godzilla do your talking for a while?"

Alvaro splayed his free hand across Cande's taut lower belly and thrust his saliva-slick rod between Cande's legs. Cande wrapped his fist around the tip, squeezing the sensitive flesh as it emerged from the vise of his thighs. Alvaro's hand shuttled up and down Cande's cock in time with his thrusts. He'd done this a few times, but he'd never felt this sense of flawless harmony, of moving in concert with someone who was perfectly in tune with him. He was not at all surprised when Cande filled his hand with cum at the same moment that he crested; no, not surprised, but joyful, grateful, and fulfilled. With his eyes closed in ecstasy, he nuzzled at Cande's nape, kissing the smooth skin of Cande's back and shoulders. Cande nestled closer, melting in the afterglow, barely able to keep his eyes open.

"*Godzilla?*" Alvaro murmured, his voice ragged with exhaustion.

Cande smiled, but fell asleep before he could answer. Alvaro was awake for a few more minutes as he basked in the wonder of having someone to love right here in his bed, and then he drifted into sweet dreams.

chapter *Seven*

WHEN Alvaro woke, he was alone. Jumping out of bed, he dragged his jeans on and flew out of his bedroom door. Cande wasn't in the bathroom or kitchen, but when Alvaro stopped his frantic search for a moment, he heard voices coming from his mother's room. He pulled the door open and saw Cande sitting in the chair beside the bed. Alvaro's mother looked at her son over the rim of her teacup, and her eyes looked brighter to him than they had in years.

"Good morning," Alvaro said.

"Good morning," Cande replied. "Would you like breakfast?"

"I don't think we have time," Alvaro said. "Why did you let me sleep so late?"

"You looked like you needed the rest." Cande smiled up at his lover, and Alvaro's cheeks turned pink.

"We should get to school," Alvaro said. "Mama, I'll be back around three, okay?"

"I'll be here," she said, smiling up at him.

"Can I get you anything before we go?"

"Cande fed and watered me. I'll be fine."

Looking a bit dazed by his mother's humor, Alvaro kissed her forehead and went to put on a shirt and shoes. Cande trailed him into his room and picked up his backpack.

"I like Marisol," Cande said. "Your mom, I mean. She said I could call her Marisol instead of Mrs. Torres."

"If that's what she said, it's fine with me." Alvaro ran a hand through his hair and grabbed his jacket off the closet doorknob. "So the two of you were talking?"

"Sort of," Cande said as they left the bedroom. "I asked if she wanted tea and ended up making breakfast. Hang on a second." He ducked into the kitchen and slid half an omelet onto a tortilla. "You can eat this on the way," he said, handing it to Alvaro.

"Thanks." Alvaro took a big bite of his portable breakfast as he opened the front door and waited for Cande to walk through. As soon as they were out of the house, he leaned toward Cande and kissed him. "I missed you when I woke up."

Cande squeezed Alvaro's shoulder. "Sorry if I made you worry."

"You don't have to apologize." Alvaro stole another kiss. "Thanks for taking care of my Mama."

"I like spending time her. She's nice and really smart."

"So what did you two talk about?" Alvaro asked as they reached the bottom of the stairs.

"She wanted to know a little bit about me."

"I wish I could tell you how happy it makes me to hear that she's interested in something."

"You just did."

Alvaro grinned at Cande. "Smart ass."

"Well, a cool guy like you would never date a dumb-ass, right?"

"You got that right." Alvaro grabbed Cande by the arm and pulled him back into the alley. Wrapping his arms around the other young man, Alvaro took his lips in sweet kiss that neither wanted to break. Alvaro slid his hands up and down Cande's back, just glorying in the reality of having this boy in his arms. As the kiss went on, one hand crept under the waistband of Cande's trousers and encountered nothing but bare skin. "Where's your underwear?" Alvaro asked.

"In my bag," Cande said breathlessly. "I've been wearing them for a couple of days, and they're getting kind of skanky."

"I could have loaned you a pair."

Cande moaned as Alvaro's fingers crept into his cleft. "Stop that. We have to go to school."

"Maybe we should just blow it off for today."

"I'd like that, but Mr. Matheson told me that if I'm absent without a reason again, I'll probably be suspended. If I'm suspended, I can't participate in any activities. If I can't participate in activities, Party of Five will be Party of Four."

"Oh." Alvaro pulled his hand from Cande's pants. "Okay. Let's get to school, but after…."

"What?" Cande pretended incomprehension as he followed Alvaro onto the sidewalk.

"I want to be alone with you."

"Really? Is there something you want to tell me in private?"

Alvaro bumped Cande's shoulder with his. "Godzilla has something he'd like to discuss with you."

Cande burst into laughter as they turned the corner. Alvaro spotted their friends waiting by the overpass. Eligio waved his arm over his head as if Alvaro couldn't see the three of them waiting on the bridge.

"You're in a good mood this morning." Kiki smirked as he knocked fists with Alvaro.

"You would be, too, if you were me," Alvaro answered.

Kiki glanced at Leo. "I wonder what could have put that grin on our Alvaro's face."

"Probably the great sex we had," Cande said.

Leo and Kiki whooped with laughter, leaning on one another to keep from falling over. Eligio gave them a disgusted look before he turned to Alvaro. "That's not really funny."

"They seem to think it is," Alvaro pointed at Leo and Kiki.

"They're weird," Eligio said. "I don't think you should let Candelario make jokes like that about you. People will get the wrong idea."

Alvaro put a hand on Eligio's shoulder. "I don't have time to explain this to you right now, but I promise I will."

Eligio gave Cande one more disapproving look before he got on his bicycle. "I'll see you guys at lunch," he said. "I promised Mr. Matheson I'd get to school a little early and help with the first year chorus."

"You're a good boy, Eligio," Kiki said, wiping tears from his eyes. Eligio gave Kiki a suspicious look, and then waved as he rode off. Kiki shook his head. "That kid is never going to believe I like him."

"Maybe because you spent so much time dissing him?" Leo said.

"I had help," Kiki answered.

"Yeah. Good times," Leo said, holding up his hand for Kiki to slap. He wrapped his fingers around Kiki's and held them for a few seconds before letting go.

"Am I missing something here?" Alvaro asked. "Since when do you two hold hands?"

"Maybe you aren't the only one who had great sex last night," Kiki replied casually, buffing his nails on his lapel.

Alvaro looked from Kiki to Leo and back again. "The two of you?"

Leo nodded, putting an arm around Kiki's shoulders. "We were going to tell you, but there hasn't been a good time."

"Wow." Alvaro looked dazed for the second time that morning. "That's... wow."

"Now we just need to find a boyfriend for Eligio," Cande said, cracking everyone up.

"You're priceless," Kiki said, throwing an arm around Cande's shoulders. Alvaro put his arm on top of Kiki's, and the four of them walked to school teasing each other the entire way. It was such heady freedom to be just themselves without having to hide anything, and the bond between them grew even stronger. They might be considered outsiders by the rest of the school, but when they were together, everyone else was an outsider.

"I FOUND a red gangster hat," Kiki told Alvaro as they walked into Mr. Cruz's classroom later that day. "With Leo's red vest, Eligio's red sneakers, and your red tie, we're all set with our stage costumes except for Cande."

"My mama has a long red scarf that I don't think she'll mind loaning him," Alvaro said, smiling at Cande. "Since they're best friends forever now."

"That's great," Kiki said as Mr. Cruz walked in and sat down at his desk. "We're all set, then. We know our routine, and we still have two days to practice."

"First prize is ours," Leo declared.

"I like your confidence," Alvaro said. "I wish Mama could be there to see us."

"Why can't she?" Cande asked.

"She hasn't left the apartment in over three years," Alvaro told him. "She barely leaves her bed except to go to the bathroom."

"Have you asked her if she'd like to go?"

"I don't even know if she knows about the festival. I've mentioned it, but it didn't seem to sink in."

"I think you should ask her. Or I could ask her, if you want."

Alvaro smiled at Cande, not quite daring to touch him in class, afraid he wouldn't be able to stop. "Would you? She actually seems to hear you when you talk."

"Hey, what's Mr. Montero doing here?" Leo whispered loudly as the classroom door opened and the headmaster entered.

Alvaro was still looking at Cande and saw his lover's expression change drastically. He glanced up and saw that the headmaster wasn't alone. Accompanying him was the big man Alvaro had seen at Cande's house. "Is that Mr. Simenon?" he asked.

Cande nodded, his eyes never leaving the head of the halfway house. He and the rest of the class watched as the headmaster spoke with Mr. Cruz. Mr. Cruz looked over the classroom until his gaze found Cande. "Candelario Carlisle, please come to the front," the teacher said.

"It's okay," Cande said softly to Alvaro. "This is just about me being out all night. No big deal."

"That's crap," Alvaro hissed. "I'm not letting you go with him."

"There's nothing you can do except get yourself in trouble. I'll see you later at practice." Cande slung his backpack over his shoulder and walked to the front.

"Carlisle, you're excused from class," Mr. Cruz said. "Go with the headmaster."

"So you think the rules are for everyone but you," Mr. Simenon said. "I can see I've given you too much slack. You need another lesson in obedience. Maybe losing your privileges wasn't enough of a wake-up call for you."

Leo and Kiki each grabbed one of Alvaro's arms and kept him in his seat. "No," Kiki whispered. "Not now. Cande's right; you won't be helping him if you get yourself in trouble."

"Yeah," Leo said. "Wait until after class and we'll go with you."

Alvaro seethed, but he knew they were right. Mr. Cruz would take great delight in assigning him detention. He could skip it, but he didn't want to do anything that would prevent Party of Five from performing at the festival. Torn, he watched Cande follow Mr. Simenon and the headmaster out the door.

"Is there a problem, Mr. Torres?" Mr. Cruz asked.

"Several," Alvaro answered as the door closed. "But I don't expect help from you."

More than one student gasped at this blatant disrespect, and Mr. Cruz's face went slack with shock. "Would you like me to call Mr. Montero back?" the teacher said.

"No."

"Then I suggest you use another tone when you speak to me. Class, you can all thank Mr. Torres for this pop quiz. Everyone take out a sheet of paper." His words were greeted with a chorus of groans, and Alvaro collected several nasty looks.

As soon as the bell rang for lunch, Alvaro was out the door with Leo and Kiki on his heels. Mr. Cruz called after them, but they pretended not to hear. They didn't slow down until they reached the quad. "Where exactly are we going?" Kiki asked.

"To make sure Cande's all right," Alvaro answered.

"Yeah, I get that," Kiki said, "but where?"

"I know where he's staying." Alvaro explained briefly.

"That's a tough neighborhood," Leo said.

"And?" Alvaro replied.

"Are you sure that's where Cande is?" Kiki asked.

"Where else would that asshole take him?"

"How would I know?"

Alvaro heard the exasperation in his friend's voice. "Sorry if I'm being a pain in the ass. I'm really worried about Cande."

Kiki and Leo closed in from either side to flank Alvaro. Each put a hand on one of Alvaro's shoulders in a show of support. Eligio gave them a puzzled look as he stopped his bike beside them. "What's going on?" he asked.

"The head of Cande's halfway house came and took him out of class," Kiki said.

Eligio looked warily at Alvaro. "You're not thinking about doing anything foolish, are you? The festival is tomorrow night."

"Thanks for the news flash, Elly," Leo said.

"Promise me you guys won't do anything to get us kicked out of the competition."

"Sorry, Elly," Alvaro said. "I can't leave Cande in that place."

"Will you wait 'til I go get Mr. Matheson?"

Alvaro chewed his lower lip in indecision. "All right," he said. "But you'd better be fast."

Eligio spun his bike around and rode off without another word. He found Mr. Matheson where he'd left him at the other end of the quad. When Eligio explained the problem, Mr. Matheson amazed him by climbing onto the back of the bicycle. Alvaro, Leo, and Kiki looked equally surprised to see a teacher in such an undignified position as Eligio braked to a stop. "Thank you for waiting," Mr. Matheson said as he dismounted and straightened his jacket. "If you can be patient for a bit longer, I'll go to the halfway house after school."

"I can't wait that long," Alvaro said.

"I can't just walk away from my classes," the music teacher said.

"I know I don't have proof, but I'm sure this guy that's in charge is beating Cande. I can't stand by while he's being hurt."

"I know how you feel. If Cande is being mistreated and he's injured while I delay, I'll never forgive myself, but—"

"What about the cop?" Alvaro interrupted. "Can you call him?"

"Cop?"

"Cande's working with a detective to get evidence on this guy that's abusing people at the halfway house."

Mr. Matheson pushed his glasses up his nose, his expression skeptical. "Do you know this policeman's name?"

"Lopez."

"I don't suppose you have a first name? There's probably more than one Officer Lopez in L.A."

Alvaro dropped his head, willing his distracted brain to work. "Pelayo!" he spit out. "The cop's name is Pelayo Lopez."

"All right, if you'll give me a few minutes, I'll go to the office and call the po—" Mr. Matheson paused as Kiki thrust a cell phone at him. "Thank you," he said, taking the phone. "I suppose I should get one of these eventually." After a few seconds of fiddling around, he handed the phone back and let Kiki key in the necessary numbers. With a nod of thanks, he raised the phone to his ear. After several short conversations, he was finally connected to the right extension. As briefly as possible, he explained the situation and hung up. "Officer Lopez is on his way to the halfway house," he told Cande's friends. "Alvaro! Where are you going?"

"Why are you asking me something you already know?"

"Let the police handle it," Mr. Matheson said.

"I will. I just have to be there."

"I know you want to, but it's really not a good idea," the teacher said. "The best thing you can do right now is go to your classes and then to practice with your friends as if everything is normal. Let the police do their job. Detective Lopez promised to let me know what happens."

"Then you'd better keep the phone," Kiki said. "Come on, man," he continued, as he took Alvaro's arm. "I know how you feel. I want to go, too, but Mr. Matheson is right. There's nothing we can do for Cande. All we can do is get ourselves in trouble and lose out on performing at the festival."

"I don't care about that!" Alvaro said, yanking his arm out of Kiki's grasp. He turned to walk away and caught sight of Eligio's face. The younger boy's look of betrayal shamed Alvaro to his core, but how could he stay here when Cande was in trouble?

Seeing Alvaro's hesitation, Mr. Matheson spoke again. "I know it's hard to trust in others, but sometimes you have to. It's a hard lesson of growing up that we can't always rescue the ones we care about. Sometimes we have to leave it to others who are better qualified. You wouldn't try to perform surgery on Cande, would you?"

It was several moments before Alvaro answered. "It would depend on the operation," he said. After another minute, Kiki smiled and then chuckled. His nervous laughter infected the others, and Alvaro waited for the gust of tension-relieving humor to blow itself out before he spoke again. "You might have to tie me to a chair to keep me here."

"I've had dreams about doing that very thing." Kiki grinned.

Leo put an arm around Alvaro's shoulders. "Seriously, man, I know how you feel. If someone threatened any one of you, I'd be out for blood, you know? But I think Mr. Matheson is right too. We can't win this one with our fists."

"How long have we been dreaming about winning this prize?" Kiki asked. "I believe you feel something really special for Cande, but just think about what he'd want you to do. Would he want you to throw it away for him?"

Grudgingly, Alvaro shook his head. "He'd be mad at me."

"He's not the only one," Eligio spoke up. "I know how gay it sounds, but you've been my hero since I was eight. The guy I look up to would never put himself before his friends."

Alvaro reached out and put a hand on the back of Eligio's neck. "I'm not going to let you down," he said, giving the younger boy's neck a squeeze. "But Cande's my friend, too, *comprende*?"

"No, I don't understand," Eligio replied, but the sharpness was gone from his voice. "We've known you a lot longer, but you treat him really special, like you like him better than us. I just don't get it."

"Elly," Alvaro began when the bell rang for the end of lunch.

"Go to your classes," Mr. Matheson said. "If Detective Lopez hasn't called me in an hour, I'll call him again."

"I don't know if I can sit in class," Alvaro said honestly. "I'm too keyed up to be still."

Mr. Matheson debated for a moment before taking a pen and pad from his jacket pocket. He wrote a note and handed it to Eligio. "Take this to the headmaster's office for me. Give it to Mr. Montero and then come to class. Thank goodness you have Music next. The rest of you get to class. If Mr. Montero grants my request, you'll all be told to report to the auditorium."

"Why?" Kiki asked.

"I'm hoping our headmaster is sincere in his statements that this school exists to help young people make something of their lives. If so, he won't mind excusing you from classes for the rest of the day and tomorrow so you can practice, win first prize, and bring glory to the school."

"Wow, that's...." For once, Kiki didn't know what to say.

"That's big," Leo finished for him. "Really big. Huge."

"It's massive," Alvaro said. "I don't know how we can thank you."

"You could take first place," Mr. Matheson answered. "And let me bask in a little of that reflected glory."

"You got it, man!" Leo said, holding up his hand.

Mr. Matheson stared at Leo's hand for a moment before he realized what Leo was doing. Solemnly, he raised his hand to touch palms in a high five. "Go on now," he said. "And try to think positively."

Alvaro and Kiki split from Leo at the door of the vocational-education building and went to their geography class. Kiki took notes on the lesson while Alvaro stared out the window until a message came over the intercom. Alvaro was on his feet and halfway to the door when the instructor excused him and Kiki to report to the auditorium. Leo caught up with them as they left the building, and they walked together. When they reached the auditorium, Eligio was waiting to let them in.

"Mr. Matheson said he'd be here as soon as class lets out," Eligio said.

"Did the cop call?" Alvaro asked.

"I don't know. Mr. Matheson put the phone in his office."

"Damn it! I should've just followed Cande."

Kiki patted Alvaro's back. "No, you did the smart thing, brother, the right thing. Don't punish yourself for it."

"I told him I'd be there for him."

"You might not believe it, but you're doing what's best for him by staying here and staying out of trouble," Leo said. "Don't you think I wanted to stay with my brother and take care of him? I had to let him stand on his own, and I had to change my ways. Do you think it was easy for me?"

Alvaro shook his head.

"Damn right it wasn't," Leo said, slapping Alvaro's shoulder. "But you know what got me through it? It was your friendship and the example you gave me."

"What are you talking about?"

"The way you took over when your mama stopped taking care of you. You just stepped up and started taking care of her. You never expected help. You never made a big deal out of it or looked for any thanks. That's huge in my eyes."

"What choice did I have?"

"The fact that you didn't see a choice is what makes you *you*," Kiki said. "And one of the many reasons that I love you."

"Hey, come on," Eligio broke in. "That's enough mushy talk."

Seeing a chance to distract Alvaro, Kiki deliberately baited Eligio. "You think this is mushy talk? You haven't heard anything yet." Leaning his cheek against Alvaro's, he spoke in a baby voice. "Oh my sweet Alvaro, I love you so so much. You are my big doughnut. You're so sweet I could eat you with a spoon. Kiss me, sugar lips."

"Stop it!" Eligio put his fingers in his ears. "Why do you guys have to joke around like that? It's disgusting!"

Alvaro exchanged a glance with Kiki. "I think I need to have a talk with Eligio," he said. "It might not be the best time, but—"

Kiki put a hand over Alvaro's mouth. "No! Wait until after the competition. I'm begging you." Alvaro nodded and Kiki moved his hand. "Thanks," Kiki said. "It's just that this is going to be a bombshell for Eligio; I don't think life-altering is too strong a term. Who knows how it'll affect his performance?"

Alvaro closed his eyes briefly and then fixed them on Kiki. "This competition has taken over our lives," he said. "It'd better be worth it."

"It's whatever we make of it," Kiki said. He looked up as Mr. Matheson entered. "He's early; the bell hasn't—" The end of his sentence was drowned out as the bell rang.

"Gentlemen," Mr. Matheson said. "I've heard from the police. I'm afraid this is a case of good news and bad news."

"How is Cande?" Alvaro asked.

"Cande is fine," the music teacher said. "Detective Lopez caught Mr. Simenon in the act of assaulting him and arrested the bastard. Cande was checked out at an emergency room, and he has no serious injuries."

"Where is he?" Alvaro asked.

Mr. Matheson pressed his lips together. "I'm afraid he's being transferred."

"Transferred!" All four young men spoke at once.

"It seems the police no longer need him here and are assigning him elsewhere."

"They can't!" Eligio said. "We need him *here*."

"They can do whatever they want; they're the police," Leo said sourly.

"Did you tell the policeman about the festival?" Eligio asked the teacher.

"The detective was very brief on the phone," Mr. Matheson said. "He seemed busy and not overly inclined to pass the time with me."

"Call him," Alvaro said.

"Please call him, sir," Eligio added.

"I'll do anything within reason to help," the teacher said, taking Kiki's phone from his pocket. "I'm just not sure this will help. The detective didn't sound very sympathetic. Hold on; he's answering. Hello, Detective Lopez. I'm sorry to bother you." Mr. Matheson walked a few feet away and turned his back.

"This isn't fair," Eligio fumed. "We changed the choreography to include five. They can't take Cande. Besides, I like him. He always understands what I mean when we talk about music. And he never teases me."

"Wait until he knows you a little better," Kiki said. "He'll find reasons to tease you."

Alvaro's lips twitched, but he kept his smile under control. "Now isn't a good time for teasing, okay? I'm trying to eavesdrop on Mr. Matheson."

The music teacher finished his conversation and turned back to the group of young men. "No promises," he said, "but Detective Lopez has agreed to meet me and talk about it some more."

"Where are we meeting him?" Alvaro asked.

"He's agreed to meet with *me*… and any other of Cande's teachers that might be interested."

"That'll be a cozy meeting," Kiki said. "Just you and the cop."

The music teacher sighed. "I'll do my best to persuade him. I'll tell him how hard you've worked and take along all the sheet music and paperwork so he'll know I'm not making it up."

"Why don't we go with you and show him?" Eligio asked.

For several moments, Mr. Matheson stared at Eligio without seeing him as he considered the notion. "That's not a bad idea," he said at last. "Loan me your phone for a bit longer, Enrique. I'll see if I can convince Detective Lopez to come here. Excuse me, please."

"What do we do in the meantime?" Alvaro asked as the teacher walked away.

"What else?" Leo said. "We practice."

For the next hour, the four young men concentrated on their dance routine with varying degrees of success. After Alvaro made the same mistake three times in a row, he stepped out of formation and called for a break. Pulling Kiki's hand to him, he looked at Kiki's watch. "I should run home and take care of Mama before too long."

Leo wiped sweat from his face with the collar of his T-shirt as he looked over at Alvaro. "You can take my hog if you want. The key's in my jacket pocket."

As Alvaro nodded his thanks, Mr. Matheson returned. "Good news," the music teacher said. "Detective Lopez has agreed to come here, and he'll bring Cande with him. So you'll have a chance to convince him that Cande should stay here."

"How did you manage that?" Kiki asked.

"I'm afraid I became somewhat emotional. I think he might have agreed to come just to end the embarrassment."

"How long before he gets here?" Alvaro asked. "I need to run home."

"I think it would take him at least an hour, maybe more," Mr. Matheson said. "But don't dawdle. You should practice as many times as possible before he gets here."

Alvaro nodded as he took Leo's keys and left the auditorium. His mother was in her usual position when he got home, but the television was off. She turned her head when he came into the room and smiled when he put the dinner tray on her lap.

"I have to go back out," Alvaro said, hoping this was one of the times when she was hearing him. "It's important or I wouldn't leave you alone for so long. You know my friend that makes the good food?"

"Honeybee," Alvaro's mother said, startling him.

"I'm talking about my friend Cande," Alvaro tried again. "He's in trouble, and I have to help him. Can you manage dinner on your own?" Alvaro's mother smiled at him again, and he took it as an affirmative. "I'll be back as soon as I can. Just put the tray on the chair when you're done eating, and I'll take care of it when I get home." Alvaro paused in the doorway. "I love you, Mama." He didn't expect an answer so he wasn't disappointed when he didn't hear one. In minutes, he was back on Leo's motorcycle on his way back to the school.

chapter Eight

ONE of the hardest things Alvaro ever did in his life was refrain from running to Cande when his friend walked into the auditorium at the policeman's side. The look on Detective Lopez's face said he wasn't in the mood for nonsense, and for once, Alvaro took a hint. However, there was no way to stop his gaze from running over Cande from top to bottom until their eyes met. All of Alvaro's love and concern shone in his gaze as he silently inquired if Cande was all right. Cande gave Alvaro a slow wink before glancing up at the policeman to see if he was being watched. Detective Lopez's attention was on Mr. Matheson as the music teacher greeted him.

"Thank you for coming," Mr. Matheson said. "We all greatly appreciate the trouble you've taken to meet with us here."

The policeman's expression was dubious as he looked around at the teenagers. Alvaro was still staring at Cande. He'd never seen the other boy in anything but a school uniform, and he was riveted by the way Cande's clinging long-sleeved T-shirt and skintight jeans accentuated his lithe limbs. Alvaro couldn't take his eyes off Cande until Kiki touched his arm. "What?" he asked as Kiki nodded toward the policeman.

"I was just saying hello," Detective Lopez said. "Remember me?"

"Yeah, I remember you," Alvaro said. "Nice to see you again, sir. Thank you for this chance."

"Nice save," Kiki whispered. "Now start paying attention. I don't care if Cande Carlisle does look like sex on a cracker."

"So what happens now?" the policeman asked loudly.

"Well, I was going to give you another version of the semi-hysterical speech you heard over the phone," Mr. Matheson said, "but I don't want you to leave. I was hoping that some of the other teachers I contacted would show up, but I guess they're busy. So I think it would be best to just let the boys show you how hard they've worked for this. They're very talented."

"I'm already familiar with some of their talents," Detective Lopez said. "I did a little research on each of these kids when Cande started hanging around with them. Not exactly a bevy of blushing virgins, are they?" He glanced at Cande. "But then again, neither is Mr. Carlisle."

"Oh dear," Mr. Matheson said. "I really hope you aren't one of those close-minded cynics who won't even give a young person a chance."

"I'm here, aren't I?" Detective Lopez looked around again. "But I have to tell you that it's going to take a lot to convince me to let Cande go. He can go places that no cop can go, making him very useful to me as an informant."

"What sort of life is that?" Everyone turned as a newcomer joined the conversation.

"Mr. Cruz?" Mr. Matheson said in surprise. "I thought you said you didn't have time for this."

"I finished grading the tests more quickly than I'd thought I would," Mr. Cruz said. "I hope you'll pardon me, but I couldn't help overhearing as I came down the aisle. Informing on criminals is not the kind of job that's going to lift a young man out of the low life."

Alvaro and his friends exchanged open-mouthed glances of shock at the unprecedented sight of Mr. Cruz speaking on behalf of a student.

"You're one of Cande's teachers?" Detective Lopez asked.

"I have Candelario, Alvaro, Enrique, and Leo in one of my classes."

"Favorites of yours, are they?"

"Hardly." Mr. Cruz sniffed. "Until about a week ago, I wouldn't have given two damns for any of them. Just a bunch of punks headed down a dead-end street."

"Don't tell me; let me guess. Something wonderful and unexpected happened to restore your faith in mankind, and you changed your mind," Detective Lopez said.

"Actually, someone simply reminded me of how I used to feel about kids who need a break. So I got off my butt and found out a little more about the punks I held in such disdain. I don't know a lot about Cande Carlisle, but I know enough about these other boys to know that they're worth at least a few minutes of my time and a good word." Mr. Cruz paused and gave the policeman a sour look his students recognized well. "Though I don't know how much good it will do."

Detective Lopez smiled wryly. "You're more persuasive than you might think. It's very easy to see people in black and white, as good or bad, but the reality is always a lot more complicated. I have to remind myself of that fact every day on the job… and still I forget. Sometimes we all need a good swift kick to the head, no matter where it comes from."

"All these boys want is a chance to compete at the festival tomorrow night," Mr. Matheson said. "They've worked very hard on their act, and it would be a shame if they had to perform without one of their members."

"You really think they have a chance of winning?"

Mr. Matheson nodded. "I know I'm just a high school music teacher, but I know talent when I see and hear it. These kids have what it takes, and if they win, they win a lot more than a trophy. Scouts from recording companies always attend this competition looking for fresh talent. These boys have a real chance at a better life if they impress the right person."

"And they're too short to play pro basketball, right?" Detective Lopez rolled his eyes. "Okay, then, let's see what they've got."

As soon as Alvaro heard the tacit permission, he beckoned to Cande. Cande came quickly to Alvaro's side and accompanied him onto the stage with the others. While Mr. Matheson showed Mr. Cruz and the policeman to the best seats, Eligio hurried to reset the music. When Eligio returned, he joined the circle the other four had made. Alvaro took Cande's hand in his right and Eligio's in his left. Each of the others joined hands, and they stood for a moment in silent communion. "Okay, *mi hermanos*," Alvaro said. "Let's kick some ass."

Detective Lopez sat between Mr. Matheson and Mr. Cruz and watched in growing amazement as Party of Five performed. The song and dance routine was as good as anything he'd ever seen. He was frankly astonished at the level of talent displayed, especially since he'd expected some half-assed gang-style posturing to accompany a piece of angry rap music. When the song ended, there was a moment of silence that Mr. Matheson quickly filled. "Of course, they aren't wearing their costumes, but I think you can get an idea of—"

"Relax," Detective Lopez said. "I'm impressed."

"So am I," Mr. Cruz said. "They sound very professional." He paused. "I've always liked that song."

Mr. Matheson covered his surprise at finding Mr. Cruz was a fan of Madonna. "May I assume Cande will be given permission to perform?"

The policeman nodded. "You're right, Mr. Matheson. It would be a real shame if these kids didn't get to compete. In fact, it looks to me as though our district might actually produce a winner this year. That would be nice. I'd love to have bragging rights over those assho—ah, those jerks in South Central."

"Thank you for your vote of confidence," Mr. Matheson said. "If you're not busy tomorrow evening, maybe you'll come to the festival."

Detective Lopez shrugged and then gestured to Cande to join him. He wasn't surprised when Alvaro came along. "Candelario Carlisle, you've been a major pain in my ass, but you helped me bust a particularly nasty piece of work. I'll make it my business to see that Mr. Simenon is never allowed to work with kids again." He paused. "I could really use your help with breaking up that prostitution ring operating in the foster care system."

"I know." Cande dropped his head. "But I've been doing this for almost two years. I need a vacation or something."

Detective Lopez's lips curved in a faint smile. "We really put you through the wringer, didn't we? I just hope you understand how important it was."

"You needed to catch some bad guys, and I was handy." Cande shrugged.

"Yeah, and maybe I got so focused that I let myself be blinded to a few things... like how young you are." Detective Lopez cleared his throat. "You held up your end of the bargain, Carlisle, and I think you've paid your debt."

"What does that mean exactly?" Alvaro asked.

"I wasn't talking to you, but it means that I'm going to request that Cande be released from any obligations to the state's attorney's office. As his primary handler, my word should be good enough to get immediate action."

"But what exactly *does* that mean?" Cande asked.

"Well, since you're eighteen, it means that you'll be cut loose."

"No probation?" Cande's tone was more than mildly suspicious.

"I think two years is enough penance. I *will* need to know where you're staying, though, for the inevitable paperwork."

"He can stay with me," Alvaro said immediately.

"Alvaro Esteban Torres," Detective Lopez, said as though he were reading his words off a mental index card. "Your mother draws a monthly disability check that's your only income. Do you really think you can take care of her and Carlisle too? Because I'm here to tell you that he's fairly high maintenance."

"Since we're both eighteen, it really isn't anyone else's business," Alvaro answered.

"You don't like me, do you?" the policeman said.

"You put Cande in danger."

"He volunteered, and, as you pointed out, he's eighteen."

"You're right," Alvaro said. "I don't like you."

"I guess I'll just have to live with that." Detective Lopez turned to Mr. Matheson and Mr. Cruz. "Thanks for an entertaining evening," he said. "Good luck to everyone tomorrow."

Cande watched the policeman walk away as though Lopez might change his mind at any moment. He jumped when Alvaro's hands wrapped around his wrist and upper arm in wordless support, prepared to hold onto him if anyone should try and take him away. "I can't believe it's finally over," Cande whispered.

"Why not? Wouldn't that be nicer than believing that it isn't over?"

"Why do you always have to make so much sense?"

Alvaro was happy to see the upward curve of Cande's lips. "Try looking on the bright side for a while and see what happens. You can always go back to being mopey if it doesn't work out."

"Hey!" Eligio yelled. "Earth to Alvaro and Cande! Are we through for the day or are we going to keep practicing like we're supposed to?"

Alvaro grinned at Eligio. "Are you saying it's time to separate the men from the boys?"

"If the rest of you think you're up to it," Eligio answered.

There was a chorus of whooping laughter as Eligio's friends fell out, Kiki actually falling to the floor to roll around helplessly. "Go, Elly!" Leo said, knocking fists with the younger boy as he grinned at Eligio's newfound cockiness. It was clear that their junior member wasn't going to let them get away with any slack behavior when it came to the act.

"I don't think they need us anymore," Mr. Matheson said to Mr. Cruz.

"Wait, sirs," Cande called out. "I want to thank both of you for speaking up for me, especially since there really isn't anything in it for you."

"It's strange," Mr. Matheson said. "But whenever I do something for nothing, I find I get my biggest rewards. I can't explain it, but it's true."

"Just don't make us look like fools, Mr. Carlisle," Mr. Cruz added. "Do your best at the competition and do your best to stay out of trouble."

Cande nodded. "Thank you both," he said again.

As the teachers walked away up the aisle, Alvaro leaned closer to Cande, stroking his arm. "I'm really glad you're back and you're all right."

"I couldn't let you guys perform without me. What chance would you have?" Cande's smile was half-hidden as he looked down at their entwined fingers, hidden behind Alvaro's thigh.

"I don't know about them"—Alvaro jerked his chin at the other three—"but I'd be lost without you."

"You say the craziest things."

"Only to you."

Cande looked up at Alvaro and their eyes locked. Alvaro leaned slowly toward Cande, like a sunflower turning to the light.

"Hey!" Eligio yelled. "No more fooling around. We need to practice!"

"It's not my fault," Alvaro responded. "If you don't want any fooling around, then tell Cande not to wear such tight clothes. How can I focus when he looks so hot?"

Eligio's blush was immediate and vivid.

Kiki rubbed his chin as he pretended to study Eligio's face. "Is it some sort of giant, radioactive strawberry?" he wondered aloud.

Leo chuckled. "No, strawberries are sweet. I think it's a mutated radish."

"It's not funny!" Eligio said through clenched teeth.

"Stop teasing him!" Cande said, coming over to stand beside Eligio. "I know you guys tease each other all the time and it's just your way of showing your love, but Elly doesn't understand that. When you pick at him, it just embarrasses him and hurts his feelings."

"Whoa!" Leo recoiled in exaggerated fear, moving behind Kiki and clinging to his back. "Save me!"

"Easy there, Mama Bear," Kiki said to Cande. "We're sorry we picked on the baby. Please spank us."

"Can't you be serious for two minutes?" Eligio asked. His tone was exasperated, but his lips wanted to spread in a smile. "Let's get to work."

"You heard the man," Alvaro said. "Let's get to work."

AFTER practice was over, Alvaro and Cande said good night to the others and began the walk to Alvaro's house. They stopped as usual on the walkway over the multiple railroad tracks, and Alvaro pulled Cande into his arms. "I'm so happy you're here," he said in Cande's ear.

Cande hugged Alvaro back. "I'm really happy too. Before we go into all the gory details of what happened while we were apart—if we even have to—could you kiss me just once?"

"For as long as you want," Alvaro said as his lips covered Cande's. He knew it had only been a few hours since he'd last kissed this boy, but his anxiety had made it seem like years. He'd had to consider the possibility that he might not see Cande again, and now Cande was in his arms, warm and unharmed, lush lips parting to welcome him. Alvaro gathered Cande closer, nearly lifting him from the ground as their tongues slid together in a wet and tender caress. Cande put his arms around Alvaro's neck, breaking the kiss as he pulled himself up to perch on the concrete railing with his feet dangling. Alvaro moved eagerly between Cande's thighs, capturing his mouth again. Cande moaned softly as Alvaro's hands slid down his sides to rest on his upper thighs. Alvaro squeezed the hard muscles, his thumbs rubbing up and down the creases where Cande's legs joined his torso. Cande reached down to cup Alvaro's crotch, fondling the rapidly hardening shaft through soft denim. Alvaro moaned into Cande's mouth as the teasing little touches brought him quickly to the brink. "I really missed you," Alvaro murmured. "And not just because of this," he added, as he nibbled at Cande's bottom lip.

"I thought about you the whole time and not just because of this," Cande replied, squeezing the bulge in Alvaro's trousers. He stopped talking as his boyfriend yanked him off the rail to straddle his thigh. He pressed his lips to Alvaro's lips, his crotch to Alvaro's hard-muscled thigh and began to rock against him in long, slow sinuous thrusts that involved his entire body. Alvaro stood firm, meeting Cande halfway but never attempting to take compete control, at least not until the very end. Pushing Cande back against the safety barrier, Alvaro re-aligned their bodies so their cocks could rub together. Once more, they fell into an effortless rhythm, welded at the mouth and groin, moving in tandem, helping one another achieve a much-desired goal. "Varo," Cande gasped as the friction and the long deep kisses wrought a minor miracle. Alvaro had no breath for words as his orgasm hit him like a heavyweight contender. The sensation was so intense that his vision went grainy and he actually saw a swarm of tiny stars for a split second. Breathing hard, he clutched at the cold concrete with both hands, leaning his forehead against Cande's. "Damn!" He expelled a long breath.

Cande hung his arms loosely over Alvaro's shoulders. "Well said. It doesn't matter how many times I yank it to a fantasy of you, it's never even close to the real thing."

"You think about me while you're yanking it?"

"Mmm hmm," Cande said lazily. "Don't you think about me?"

"Well sure, but I didn't know you did the same thing."

"Why wouldn't I?"

"I don't know. I guess I just don't think of you as a grubby, dirty-minded little pervert like most of the guys I know. You're… damn, this is going to sound so lame, but you're like an angel or something to me."

Cande chuckled. "We're all grubby, dirty-minded little perverts."

"Damn, I just feel so amazingly, monumentally great right now!" Alvaro hugged Cande tight. "I don't even care that I'm going to walk home with my underwear stuck to me."

"Yuck, don't remind me. I hate cold cum."

Alvaro laughed. "Remind me never to serve you cold cum."

Cande smacked the back of Alvaro's head. "Way to ruin a perfectly good climax with a bad joke, man."

"I'll make it up to you as soon as we get home," Alvaro promised with a sweet kiss.

Cande grinned up at him, breaking the kiss. "Are you sure you'll be up to it?"

Alvaro moved away from Cande and looked him up and down. "No problem as long as you're dressed like that."

"Dressed like what?" Cande said as he straightened his clothes, plucking the front of his pants away from his crotch.

"The way you're dressed. Those pants couldn't be any tighter without cutting off your circulation."

"You don't like them?"

"Oh, I like them all right. I've just never seen you dressed like this."

"Like what?" Cande asked again.

"I'm not dissing you. It's just a surprise to see you looking so… sexy."

"You're surprised I'm sexy?" Cande's expression was impossible to read.

"I *know* you're sexy, but it surprised me to see you dressed in a sexy way. Does that make sense?"

"Do these clothes really look sexy? I mean… it's just a T-shirt and jeans."

"They do when you're wearing them. I don't think they'd do much for Mr. Cruz."

Cande gave Alvaro another smack as they started walking. "You might as well know from the start: I like clothes," he admitted as Alvaro took his hand. "I like looking at magazines and putting outfits together. The other guys at the halfway house were always on my case about how much time I spend in the bathroom, but I want to look my best when I can."

"I like the way you're dressed. By the way, where are the rest of your things?"

"I'll have to go pick them up, but I can wear this tomorrow until it's time to get into costume. That's something to worry about later. All we should be concentrating on is the competition."

"You're gorgeous *and* smart," Alvaro said, kissing the top of Cande's head. "How did I get so lucky?"

"I think I'm more of a mixed blessing."

"Not to me and I'm sure Mama's going to love having you around."

"I'll get a job," Cande said. "You don't have to worry about me being a drag on your family."

"That's something to worry about later," Alvaro said as they climbed the stairs to the apartment.

"Don't quote me to me," Cande said, poking Alvaro in the side.

Alvaro retaliated, and they spent a breathless couple of minutes making out on the stairs. "Come on," Alvaro said, pulling Cande by the hand. "Let's say good night to Mama and go up to the roof."

"You really like doing it outside, huh?"

"Never thought about it. I guess I do." Alvaro opened the door and went inside. "Are you hungry? I'm going to fix Mama a snack."

"I'll do it," Cande said. "Go on in and sit with her. Break the bad news that you took in a stray."

Alvaro grinned and threw a lazy punch at Cande that was easily dodged. "She's going to love having a full-time cook," he said as he headed down the hall.

Cande joined them in a few minutes with a vegetable salad, and they all watched a talent show that encouraged contestants to do their worst. When it was over, Alvaro and Cande excused themselves and hurried up to the roof. Cande got to the top of the fire stairs first and ran across the tarred surface to the edge. Putting out his arms at shoulder level, he leaned into the updraft, knees braced against the short wall. Alvaro came up behind Cande and put his arms around his lover's slim waist. "I'm still having a hard time believing I'm free," Cande said. "I don't have to report to anyone."

"Except Eligio," Alvaro drawled. Cande laughed, making Alvaro's heart leap. Alvaro held the other young man tighter, nuzzling at his nape. "I love you so much," he murmured.

Cande turned in the circle of Alvaro's arms and framed Alvaro's face in his hands. Looking into his boyfriend's eyes, Cande pulled his head down for a sweet, lingering kiss. Alvaro made a yummy humming noise as their lips parted. He looked so happy and satisfied that his next words came as a shock to Cande. "Are you mad at me for not coming after you?"

"What? Of course not. I'd have been mad if you *had* come after me."

"I just can't figure it out. What am I doing wrong?"

"What are you talking about?" Cande asked with a puzzled frown. "You're not doing anything wrong."

"Then why don't you love me?"

Cande looked away from Alvaro's earnest gaze. "I do."

"Then why don't you tell me?"

"Isn't the fact that I sleep with you proof enough?"

"Of course not. Anyone can have sex. I don't want to just be *amigos con derechos*; I want to know that I'm special to you."

"You are." Cande pressed his lips to Alvaro's and grabbed a handful of his crotch, willing him to stop talking.

"Shit!" Alvaro groaned. "No one makes me feel the way you do."

"I know exactly what you mean," Cande breathed against Alvaro's neck as he kissed his way south. "So why are you just standing there? We're all alone, and we're both hard again."

"I don't know. It isn't like me to waste an opportunity, but...." Alvaro concentrated his gaze on the lock of red-blond hair that fell over Cande's left eye. Gently, he brushed it back, letting his fingers trail over the silken skin beneath. "I just have this weird feeling like... like... what's the point, you know?"

Cande blinked in astonishment. "The point? It's sex, Alvaro, casual sex."

"It's not casual to me. Not anymore. If it ever was."

"So are you saying you don't want to make out with me?"

"Of course I do. Are you kidding? I just want to know that we're on the same wavelength."

"The same wavelength?" Cande put his palms against Alvaro's chest and pushed away from him. "Am I going to have to fit into some picture you have of how things should be?"

"No! I just want—"

"You just want me to live by your rules." Cande shook his head. "Man, I never thought you'd pull this shit, not you. Wow, you had me completely fooled. When am I going to learn?"

"Cande, wait!" Alvaro called out as Cande walked toward the stairs. When his boyfriend didn't slow down, Alvaro followed. By the time he caught up, Cande was in his mother's room. Alvaro knocked and was told to go away. Deciding that Cande could use a few minutes to calm down, Alvaro went into the kitchen to get a soda.

"WHAT'S the matter, honeybee?" Mrs. Torres asked as Alvaro's steps faded down the hall.

Cande shrugged and tried to change the subject. "I think it's cool that you can talk but you only do it when you want to," he said. "People tend to leave you alone."

"You—" She paused to moisten her lips. "You misunderstand."

"I'm sorry. I wasn't saying that your... illness isn't real."

"I know you weren't."

"Will you tell me what it is that I don't understand?"

"I didn't choose silence. Many times I've wanted to talk, but I just... I couldn't find the strength. I didn't choose to cut myself off from the world, but somehow that's what happened." She took a deep breath. "It's not a good thing, honeybee."

"I could understand if you wanted to, though." Cande dropped his eyes. "The world can be really harsh."

"I know. It's hard to lose what we love."

"How do you know what I'm thinking? It's kind of spooky."

"I know what you're feeling," Mrs. Torres corrected. "But I won't know what your problem is unless you tell me."

"How could Alvaro possibly know he loved me at first sight?" Cande asked baldly.

Alvaro's mother didn't flinch at the revelation that her son loved a boy, nor did she hesitate with her answer. "How does a mother know at first sight that she'll love her child all her life? Some things can't be explained with words and don't need to be."

"I feel like I'm getting something for nothing, and it makes me nervous. I feel like Alvaro's making a mistake in being my friend. I'm afraid he'll wise up and run away as fast as he can. And I'll be alone again feeling like the world's biggest idiot for even thinking I deserved him."

"Alvaro's father used to say something like that: that you don't get something for nothing in this world."

"I didn't mean to remind you of something sad."

"Don't worry about that. I treasure my memories of Alvaro's father. He tried very hard to take care of his family, to do what was expected of him, but he was... well, he was trying to be something he wasn't and it... twisted him into a bad shape. I live in the past most of the time because it's a pleasant place for me, the time when Alberto loved me and we were a family. It's Alvaro who can't bear to remember." Mrs. Torres sighed. "It's funny when you think about it... how very ordinary everything is and how very special at the same time." When Cande gave her a puzzled look, she turned her head on the pillow to look out of the window. "This has been my view for a long time now," she said. "Part of a wall, a sliver of the street, and a glimpse of the tree on the other side. The same every day, but changing by small degrees until summer becomes autumn, and then winter and so on. But it's such a comfort to know that every day the light will change in the same way and that it will gradually become dark and then light again when the sun rises. And the light on the leaves of that tree...." Tears trembled on edges of her eyelids. "The light makes everything so beautiful. If we just could appreciate each moment for the miracle it is, we'd never know regret." Mrs. Torres sighed again. "But we're not made that way. Maybe we're just too weak to bear so much beauty, and so we trivialize things and memories fade." Her voice trailed off into several moments of silence.

Cande cocked his head at her. "You don't sound like someone who doesn't care about anything to me. It's more like you care too much."

"I don't want you to be someone who doesn't care. Don't push away love just because it hurts sometimes. It's worth the pain." She reached out to touch Cande's cheek. The warm motherly touch melted several defensive layers, and Cande slumped in the chair with his head hanging low. Alvaro's mother stroked his hair as he struggled with his tears. "You're never too old to cry, *mijo*," she said.

Cande dragged his sleeve across his eyes. "I don't want to be sad right now," he said. "I'm free. I have a place to live with people who have the bad sense to like me. I have a very big day tomorrow. I want to be excited and happy about these things."

"I won't stop you."

Cande looked at her in surprise.

Mrs. Torres smiled. "The only one stopping you is you."

Cande stood and kissed her cheek. "I'll try to be more… open," he said. "Thank you for talking to me, Marisol."

"You might get tired of my voice now that I've found it again."

"Never. Good night," Cande said, smiling as he closed the door. Seeing the light in the kitchen, he went to find Alvaro. When Cande walked in, Alvaro looked up from a huge bowl of leftover rice and spicy shredded pork. A few grains of rice were stuck to a smear of sauce on his upper lip, and Cande reached out to wipe them off with his thumb. "What a pig," Cande said. "Do I have to get you a bib?"

"You're not mad at me anymore?"

"I wasn't mad at you."

"Oh." Alvaro took another bite, chewed, and swallowed. "Are you sure? 'Cause you sounded mad to me."

"So you're drowning your sorrow in food? Do you know how many calories are in that?"

"You're trying to depress me, aren't you?"

Cande shook his head. "I'm trying to show you that I love you."

Alvaro sat up a little, as he set his bowl on the counter. "I'm sorry; I don't think I heard you right. Did you say that you love me?"

"You want me to repeat it?"

"Yes, could you? I'd really like that."

"I don't know why I'd love a jerk like you, but I do. I mean… I must love you or I wouldn't be acting like such a fool."

"Are you acting like a fool?"

"Yeah. I'm trusting someone not to hurt me. It hasn't worked out too well in the past."

"I wasn't in your past."

"Do most people find your cockiness attractive?"

"What? You don't?"

Cande pretended to think about it. "It amuses me," he said at last.

"Is that so? Then why aren't you laughing?" With no warning, Alvaro lunged, fingers dancing over Cande's ribs, finding his lover's ticklish places. Cande collapsed in helpless laughter, taking both of them to the floor with a loud thump. They leaned together, stifling their giggles as they listened for noise from Alvaro's mother's room. "I'm hard again," Alvaro whispered.

Cande checked for himself. "So," he said in dramatic tones, "Godzilla rises once more to terrorize an unsuspecting world."

Alvaro stood and pulled Cande to his feet, groping his crotch in the process. "Does this mean you're interested in fooling around a little more?" he asked, squeezing his boyfriend's half-hard cock. He slid his other hand under Cande's armpit and dug in with his fingertips. Cande bit his bottom lip to hold in his giggles and beat weakly at Alvaro with both hands. Alvaro showed no mercy, holding Cande up with an arm around his back as he tickled him. When he finally relented, his lover was flushed, hiccupping, and limp in his arms. Scooping Cande up, Alvaro carried him to his bedroom and put him on the bed. He unfastened Cande's snug trousers and freed his cock. Grabbing hold of the shaft, he took the head in his mouth, swirling his tongue around and around.

"Fuck!" Cande gasped. "That feels good."

Encouraged, Alvaro did everything he could think of to bring Cande pleasure. He licked his way down the hard shaft, yanking at Cande's pants when they hampered his access to more skin. Cande lifted his ass, and Alvaro peeled off the stretchy jeans and underwear. "Look at you," he breathed as he reached for the rosy length of Cande's arousal. "You're so beautiful." Cande fell back onto his elbows as Alvaro nuzzled at his balls while stroking his saliva-slick shaft. Alvaro licked and sucked at the tender sacs until Cande was squirming against the sheets. Raising his head, Alvaro took the tip of the rod in his mouth again. Cande grabbed a double handful of the bedding, braced the soles of his feet against the floor, and pumped his hips. Alvaro caught hold of Cande's sleek flanks, controlling his lover's wild thrusts as he took him deeper.

"Varo!" Cande said in a choked little voice. Alvaro sucked harder, releasing Cande's hips to tease his nipples with random pinches. Cande shook and moaned as the pleasant tension in his groin ratcheted ever higher until he reached the peak. "Alvaro," he breathed as his climax burst within him, and he spurted down Alvaro's throat. His muscles jerked as his boyfriend continued to go down on him, sucking until he was dry. Completely enervated by the tickling and the orgasm, Cande lay across the narrow bed like a shipwreck survivor cast up on a friendly coast.

Alvaro reluctantly allowed Cande's sated cock to slide from between his lips. He didn't feel the immediate necessity to rinse out his mouth that usually struck him after swallowing a load. The taste of semen wasn't one of his favorites, but Cande's flavor wasn't bitter or musty; Cande's cum was sort of salty and sweet at the same time. "I am such a sap," he murmured.

"Hm?" Cande purred.

"I even love the taste of your cum. How sappy is that?"

"You're king of the saps," Cande laughed softly. "But you give great head."

"You really think so?" Alvaro stretched out on top of Cande.

"The best. No one's ever done that with my nipples before. It really adds another dimension."

Alvaro tweaked Cande's nipples and his lover arched beneath him. "Pretty sensitive, aren't you?" he said as he lowered his head to take a pinkish-brown nub between his teeth. "Whoa!" Alvaro drew back as Cande nearly bucked him off. "Really sensitive."

"I came just a second ago," Cande groaned. "I'm kind of sensitive all over right now."

A wicked grin spread over Alvaro's face as he swiped his tongue over a tight nipple. Cande moaned, undulating against Alvaro, his body silently asking for more. Alvaro obliged, lavishing the attention of his lips, teeth, tongue, and fingers on Cande's nipples. Cande writhed under Alvaro's welcome weight as bolts of sheer bliss sped from two points on his chest straight to the end of his cock. None of Cande's previous lovers had been interested in anything above the waist, and Alvaro's technique was a revelation to him. In just a few minutes, the languid foreplay and the rocking of Alvaro's body against his had Cande growing hard again.

"This is fucking amazing," Cande panted. "No one's ever made me feel this good. Hell, I didn't know it was possible to feel this good."

Alvaro's chest swelled with pride as he raised his head to take Cande's lips in a passionate kiss. "Could we do what we did the other night?" he asked.

"Oh hell yes!" Cande turned on his side facing the wall. Alvaro spooned against Cande's back, hurriedly unzipping and pushing his pants down far enough to free his aching cock. "We forgot lube again." Cande chuckled before spitting in his hand. Alvaro didn't answer; he was pulling Cande's shirt up in back to bare more flesh to his mouth. Cande laughed again, as he helped Alvaro get the shirt off over his head. Clamping Alvaro's spit-slippery hard-on between his strong thighs, Cande squeezed as hard as he could. Alvaro groaned, biting down on the satiny skin of Cande's upper back as he thrust instinctively. Curving one hand around Cande's hipbone, Alvaro took hold of Cande's revived erection with the other. To an ever faster tempo, the two young men moved together, meshing smoothly in action, gliding as though they were composed of something more fluid than flesh and bone. "Don't stop," Cande whimpered, and the soft, needy sound triggered Alvaro's release. Wrapping both arms around Cande, Alvaro thrust a few more times as he pumped the quivering rod in his hand. His seed unspooled between Cande's thighs as Cande squirted a small load in his fist. "Fuck, Alvaro," Cande breathed. "Three times...."

Alvaro rubbed his cheek against Cande's nape like a drowsy lion. A shiver ran the length of Cande's frame as Alvaro's whiskers burned soft skin. Alvaro splayed a hand over Cande's lower belly, his fingers spanning the taut expanse of flesh, feeling Cande's abdominal muscles clenching in waves as the echoes of his orgasm rippled outward. Alvaro held Cande tighter, glorying in the knowledge that this was his doing. *Three times* was his last thought before he dropped off to sleep.

Cande curled his fingers around Alvaro's forearm where it crossed his chest and ignored the incipient itch of drying bodily fluids. He'd be asleep soon and it wouldn't matter. What mattered was that he wasn't alone. He had someone who truly cared about him.

"IT'S really late," Kiki said as he removed his helmet.

Leo rocked the bike onto the stand and turned to look out over the water. Moonlight glimmered on the crests of wavelets in the tiny inlet, making the swatch of ocean look like dark satin covered with silver sequins. "Yeah," he agreed. "Really late."

"We should be getting a good night's sleep to be ready for tomorrow."

"We should," Leo said, moving behind Kiki, resting gloved hands on his lover's shoulders. "I love this place at night."

Kiki twisted his neck to look at Leo. "It has a lonely feel to me."

Leo shrugged and wrapped his arms around Kiki's neck, resting his chin on Kiki's shoulder. "I come here sometimes when I can't sleep. I used to, anyway. I don't seem to have as much trouble sleeping these days."

"Because of the world-class fucking I give you every night."

"That helps and don't forget about the way I make you scream your lungs out when I'm nailing you. That's pretty tiring."

Kiki reached back and grabbed a double handful of Leo's round ass. "Exhausting," he said. "Seriously, though, you take me to the edge and beyond every time."

"Same here. If I'd known fucking guys was this good, I wouldn't have wasted so much time."

"Don't you like sleeping with girls?"

Leo shrugged again. "I manage to get off with chicks, but I can't say it thrills me. I do it mostly because I figure it's what I'm supposed to be doing. I've never thought of myself as a big player, but I never thought of myself as gay, either, you know?"

"Neither has anyone else… thought of you as gay, I mean. Funny, I actually enjoy sex with girls, but I'm the one that gets called fairy."

"You're all man, Tomas Enrique Julio Viera," Leo said. "And to be perfectly honest, I don't really want to do this with anyone but you."

"You want to be exclusive?"

"Yeah, I do." Leo turned Kiki to face him. "I want you to wear my ring," he said. "I'll have to buy one, of course."

Kiki smiled widely, his teeth gleaming white in the moonlight. "You're serious."

"Damn right I am. Why are you grinning like that?"

"I'm not laughing at you, I promise. I'm just a little amazed at how happy I feel right now. I don't have a single doubt about this."

"Why would you? We're perfect together."

"Can't argue with that, but I still have a hard time believing this is really happening. How could we see each other every day and not have a clue we felt this way?"

"Beats the crap out of me," Leo answered. "But I never claimed to be an Einstein."

"I think you'd have to be Freud to figure this one out. Hey!" Kiki abruptly switched gears. "Until we get some rings, why don't we exchange necklaces?"

"If you want, but yours is worth a lot more than mine."

"Not to me," Kiki said as he unclasped the chain from around his neck and held it out.

Leo took the heavy solid gold necklace and fastened it around his neck. The large good luck coin pendant, still warm from Kiki's body heat, lay cupped in the hollow of his collarbones. Looking into Kiki's dark depthless eyes, Leo unknotted his choker of braided leather and cowry shells. Deftly, he tied the leather lacing behind Kiki's neck as Kiki held his hair out of the way. "It looks good on you," Leo said. "Makes you look like a real surfer."

"Come on, man; I wasn't that bad on a board."

"Actually, you were pretty good," Leo said. "I just couldn't tell you back then. It would've looked like I was sucking up to the rich kid."

Kiki smiled at a memory as he mused, "Why don't we surf anymore?"

"In my case: *no tiempo, no dinero.*"

"No time, no money," Kiki repeated thoughtfully. "It's like our sixteenth summer ended and so did a way of life. Everyone's so serious now. It used to be that my parents never paid any attention to what I was doing unless I got in big trouble. Now they want to know what my college plans are, what career track I'm on." Kiki sighed. "Maybe they're just feeling guilty about the divorce and they're trying to make themselves feel less shitty by pretending to take an interest in me. But that doesn't explain everything else."

Leo took Kiki's chin on his palm, forcing his lover to meet his eyes. "Your parents are getting divorced?"

"They told me a couple of weeks ago, but I didn't want to say anything until I was sure."

"I'm sorry," Leo said, pulling Kiki into a hug.

"Yeah, me too." Kiki leaned against Leo, taking comfort in the solid warmth of Leo's body. "They weren't around that much, and when they were, they didn't have much time for me, but I liked them together, you know? They…." He paused as he tried to put his thoughts into words. "They laughed at each other's jokes," he said at last. "I know that sounds lame, but sometimes, we'd be having dinner together, and they'd start talking about some crappy book or movie that they didn't like, and they'd try to out-do each other in making fun of it. They'd have me laughing so hard that my sides hurt. I'll miss that."

"At least you'll have me."

"Don't say it like that." Kiki lifted his head to smile at Leo. "You make me laugh 'til my sides hurt too."

"Eligio's right. You can't be serious for two minutes."

"Thank you."

"*Loco*," Leo said fondly as he covered Kiki's smiling lips with his. Kiki ran his fingers through Leo's short hair, cupping the back of his head, returning the pressure of his mouth. Leo altered the angle of his chin, parting his lips for Kiki's tongue. Leo was still amazed that this boy he'd seen almost every day for four years, this boy who'd been a rival, a drinking buddy, class clown, one-third of three musketeers, this boy he seen puking his guts out, who had farted in his face, this boy was *the one*. Every time they kissed, Leo felt like he was on his motorcycle doing around one hundred and twenty miles per hour with the smell of the ocean in the wind and the sun beating down on his head and shoulders, the powerful engine vibrating between his thighs. This was how he wanted to feel for the rest of his life.

"I wish we could stay like this forever," Kiki said as he broke the kiss.

"I was just thinking that," Leo said.

Kiki kissed the end of Leo's stubbled chin. "It's all different now, isn't it?"

"Yeah, but different doesn't mean bad. Changes can be good. Remember what you said to Alvaro? That things are what we make of them?"

"I said that? I must have been high as the cost of living."

Leo punched him lightly on the chin. "It was a smart thing to say. You just need to take your own advice."

"So your advice is to take my advice?" Kiki smiled. "I'll do my best if you'll stick around and keep reminding me."

"I'll try, but I'm not as good at nagging as you are."

Kiki chuckled. "We deserve each other, but never in a million years would I have guessed we'd end up together."

"Oh come on. The poor little rich kid and the grease monkey from the wrong side of the tracks? According to the movies, we were meant to be together." Leo paused. "One of us should probably be a girl, though."

"I wouldn't look good in a prom dress."

"Liar." Leo took Kiki's mouth in a slow, sweet kiss that left them both a little breathless.

"We should go home and go to bed," Kiki said reluctantly when the kiss ended.

"Or the other way around."

"We've already done it once tonight, and I can't believe Eligio didn't catch us. I thought for sure we were going to get locked in the auditorium."

"Now you've ruined the mood. Eligio and hot sex just don't go together." Leo picked up Kiki's helmet and handed it to him.

"We can always do it again when we get home," Kiki said as he fastened his chin strap.

Leo patted the seat of the motorcycle. "Admit it; my hog turns you on."

"Of course it does," Kiki said as he climbed on behind Leo.

"Just checking," Leo said.

Kiki slipped his arms around Leo's waist as Leo twisted the throttle, revving the engine several times before he drove up onto the pavement. "You don't have to show off for me; I know what a cool guy you are," Kiki said in Leo's ear.

"Well, you might forget." Leo chuckled as the access road joined the highway, and the bike blended seamlessly with inbound traffic. Kiki leaned against his lover's back, out of the slipstream, as they picked up speed, holding tight until Leo pulled into the parking garage and shut off the engine.

As they entered the apartment building, Kiki thought about calling Alvaro's house and telling him to climb off Cande and get some rest, but he left his phone in his pocket. It wasn't as if he was setting such a good example. Eligio was probably the only one of them who'd be well rested tomorrow. Kiki's resolution to take a shower and go to sleep lasted as long as it took Leo to get in the tub with him.

"There's plenty of hot water," Kiki said lightly.

"Then we can take our time," Leo said, kissing his way across Kiki's back and shoulders. Kiki's head dropped forward as he braced his palms against the tile wall. Leo rocked against Kiki, his hard cock sliding up and down the cleft of Kiki's ass as he reached around to play with Kiki's nipples. "Do you like this?" Leo purred in Kiki's ear.

"No, I hate it," Kiki said. "You have exactly two hours to stop it."

Leo chuckled, sliding a hand down to take hold of Kiki's long cock. "I think you get bigger every time we do it," he said.

"Man, I hope not. Otherwise, I'll be dragging the ground by Monday."

"Crazy clown." Leo pumped Kiki's arousal to a faster tempo. "Let's see you laugh at this." Leaning all his weight on his lover, he pressed him to the wall, churning his hips to the same insistent rhythm. Kiki groaned as he was rocked, wet skin sliding on the tile, trusting Leo to keep him upright. Each time Leo's cock rubbed against Kiki's ass, Kiki felt a tingly little itch at his opening that added to his growing excitement. If Leo kept up this pace, Kiki was going to come in record time.

"Kiss me," Kiki said, craning his neck until Leo could access his lips. He opened his mouth to accept Leo's tongue, sucking it in as he widened his stance and shoved his butt tighter against Leo's crotch. Leo thrust harder, rubbing the fat vein on the underside of his dick between Kiki's wet, soapy cheeks, his hand working Kiki's rigid length as the hot spray bounced off their skin. Kiki's right hand curled into a fist, beating out a cadence of need on the shower wall as his lover drove him ever closer to the peak.

"Turn around." Impatiently, Leo took Kiki by the arm and turned him until they were facing each other. "Man, you are so fucking sexy," he breathed. Pushing his fingers into the wet tangled waves of Kiki's hair, he pulled his lover into a passionate kiss. Kiki moaned into Leo's mouth, and Leo took both arousals in his hand to stroke them slowly. When Kiki began to thrust, Leo stopped moving his hand and let Kiki fuck his fist. As the hard wet shaft slid against his cock, Leo thrust his tongue into Kiki's mouth at the same tempo. "Gonna come any second," he gasped as he relinquished Kiki's lips.

Kiki leaned back against the tiles, his arms spread, palms flat against the glossy surface, hips canted forward as he thrust. Leo began to shuttle his hand up and down again as he leaned to take one of Kiki's nipples between his teeth. As Leo nipped at the sensitive bud, Kiki crested with a hoarse cry, spilling his seed over Leo's knuckles. Kiki continued to pump his hips, sliding his cock against Leo's until Leo came a few strokes later. Bracing a hand against the wall, Leo took Kiki's mouth in a deep kiss as he fondled their spent cocks, his fingers moving lazily back and forth. Kiki returned the kiss, wrapping his fist around Leo's hand and stopping the repetitive motion. "*Basta...* enough," he breathed, his lips moving against Leo's.

"Are you sure? 'Cause I can go all night, you know. That's why they call me The Machine."

"They called you The Machine because you never showed any emotion in the surfing competitions. They also called you Iceman even though you're red hot."

Leo's pleased smile made Kiki's heart expand until his ribs were in danger. "I like doing it in the shower," Leo said. "It makes the clean up so much easier."

Kiki laughed softly. "I love you," he said. "Now shut up. I've just had a really intense orgasm and I want to bask."

"Wouldn't you rather bask in bed?"

"Sure, but unfortunately, I'm boneless at the moment. That's going to make walking difficult."

Leo curled his fingers around Kiki's cock again. "No you're not." Kiki grinned, and then his eyes bugged out as Leo lifted him into his arms. Dripping water all the way, Leo carried Kiki to the bedroom. Neither of them cared that they got the sheets wet. They curled up together and slept soundly through the night.

chapter Nine

ALVARO woke to the smell of frying eggs. It was a second or two before it struck him that Cande was still spooned against him. Easing out of bed, Alvaro opened his bedroom door and stuck his head out. Through the pulled back curtain in the entry to the kitchen he could see a fall of dark hair and the sleeve of a faded blue robe. "Mama?" he called out.

"Good morning," Mrs. Torres said. "I'm trying to make an omelet. Is the honeybee awake yet?"

"His name's Cande, Mama," Alvaro told her with an exasperated roll of his eyes. Then it struck him that he was having a more or less normal conversation with his mother. Shutting the bedroom door, he dressed hurriedly.

"What's the rush?" Cande inquired drowsily.

"It's my mama. She's in the kitchen."

"And?"

"I just feel like I need to check on her."

Cande smiled lazily. "I think I love you, mama's boy," he said.

Alvaro gazed down at his lover's sleep-soft body, just-been-fucked hair, and pouty mouth. He could hear his mother moving around in the kitchen and the clatter of something metal hitting the linoleum, but the allure of Cande's body was magnetic. His tongue came out to wet his lower lip as he remembered the taste of Cande's mouth. His fingertips tingled, longing to stroke the satin smoothness of Cande's skin.

"You look hungry," Cande said. "Go see what Marisol's making for breakfast."

A slow smile spread over Alvaro's face. "You have no idea how close you were to being fucked right through the mattress. Put some clothes on and come on out. You can borrow anything of mine you want."

By the time Cande was dressed, Alvaro's mother had retreated to her room again, leaving behind a savory aroma. Cande looked in on her, but she looked so tired that he left her alone. When he entered the kitchen, Alvaro was already halfway through his breakfast.

"I forgot how good her omelets are," Alvaro said.

Cande took a bite and nodded. "I love those little bits of spicy sausage and the way the onions are still crunchy."

"And the peppers, don't forget the hot peppers." Alvaro took the last bite of his eggs and eyed Cande's omelet. "You and Mama cook the same way."

"You want some of this?" Cande held out his plate, and Alvaro wasn't shy about helping himself. "I'm too excited to eat."

"That's why you're so skinny. You should learn to eat whether you're hungry or not."

"I think that's the worst advice I've ever heard."

"Wait until you've known me a little longer. I'm sure you'll hear worse." Alvaro's gaze swept down Cande's willowy frame. "You look good in my shirt, but you could have borrowed something clean."

Cande shook his head as he smoothed the front of the green and white striped jersey. "I want to wear this one."

"Suit yourself, but it must smell awful. I played a full game of soccer in it."

"It smells like you," Cande said with an embarrassed little smile.

Alvaro looked puzzled for a couple of seconds before comprehension lightened his expression. "That's really sexy," he drawled. "Can I wear your shirt?"

"I'd pay money to watch you trying to get into it."

"It's pretty tight," Alvaro said several minutes later. He'd managed to get Cande's shirt on, but he didn't think he could move his arms.

"It's like a second skin," Cande said. "Practically indecent. Don't!" he said quickly as Alvaro started to peel the shirt off. "Maybe you could just wear it until we have to leave the house?"

Alvaro circled Cande's waist with his arms. "Does it turn you on?"

"Everything about you turns me on." Cande gave Alvaro a hummingbird kiss. "But we don't have time to do anything about it. We have a competition to win, in case you forgot."

Alvaro's eyes met Cande's as the phone began to ring in the front room. "I'll bet you anything that's Eligio," Alvaro said.

"You mean Drill Sergeant Eligio?"

Alvaro chuckled as he let go of Cande and went to answer the phone. He was already hanging up when Cande came into the room. "You'll never guess," Alvaro said. "Eligio wants everyone to meet him at the auditorium as soon as possible. He can't wait until ten."

"I'm shocked."

"Grab your stuff, and we'll tell Mama and be out of here."

"Wouldn't it be great if every day was like this?" Cande said as he followed Alvaro down the short hallway. "Waking up after great sex, having breakfast, and running out the door to go sing and dance for people."

"I could stand it," Alvaro said, tossing Cande's backpack to him. "Think my clothes would fit in there too?"

"Probably." Cande put the bag on the bed and unbuckled it. He pulled out the folded square of pale blue flannel and set it on Alvaro's pillow. "If I leave this out."

Alvaro turned with his school uniform in his arms and glanced at the bed. "Are you sure? I can put these in a grocery bag."

"I want our clothes together."

"But you always carry it."

"It was my baby blanket, the only thing my mom gave me," Cande took Alvaro's clothes from him and began refolding them. "I think it's time I stopped carrying it around."

Alvaro hugged Cande from behind, squeezing him tight. "I'll be your blanket if you need one."

"Well," Cande pretended to consider, "you *are* very warm."

"And thick, don't forget."

"No you're not. You're just... you just tend to see things one way."

"Isn't that the same thing?"

"No. You're not stupid. You just think you're right all the time and you don't listen to other people." Cande took Alvaro's hands and interlaced their fingers. "It could be worse. You could be like me and never be sure if you're right."

"But this is a good thing," Alvaro said. "We'll balance each other out."

"Or make each other crazy."

"You've already made me crazy." Alvaro kissed the side of Cande's neck.

"Oh no," Cande answered, shivering at the prickle of whiskers, "you're not blaming that on me. You were crazy way before I met you."

"Maybe, but you've definitely done something with my balls."

"What?" Cande was jarred out of the sensual spell Alvaro's lips were weaving.

"I used to have balls, but since you came along, I've started listening to other people's opinions and once in a while, I actually think before I act."

"Okay, I'll take credit for you sprouting a brain. You should go shave now. I'll say goodbye to your mama for both of us. Go now."

Grumbling as he adjusted the crotch of his jeans, Alvaro went into the bathroom. He heard the door to his mother's room open, and his reflection smiled at him. His mama had actually gotten out of bed for something other than a trip to the bathroom. This morning it didn't seem beyond the realm of possibility that she might even go outside again one day soon. The odds that he might get his mother back, whole and healthy, no longer seemed so overwhelming.

Alvaro ran the razor over his chin with extra care. He had to look his very best when he went on stage. He had to sing his best and dance his best. Winning first prize had gone from being his goal in life to being one third of a trifecta of happiness that included winning Cande's love and having at least part of his family restored.

He gazed at his mirror twin as he patted his face dry and was struck by how much he resembled the picture of his father on his mother's nightstand. Alberto Alvaro Torres had been gone for half of Alvaro's life and had never been in touch, not even second hand. Alvaro had gotten along without him for this long; maybe he really didn't need him. Maybe he could stand in Alberto's place and try to do a better job of being a man. Maybe he could even understand some day how a man could walk away from his wife and child. Maybe he should have listened when his mother had tried to explain, and maybe she wouldn't have stopped talking. *Maybe.*

Cande's laugh bubbled forth down the hall, and Alvaro shook off his pensive mood. Pulling on a white tank top, he hurried down the hall to his mother's room. "Come on," he said to Cande as he entered. "Eligio's going to have an aneurysm."

"Alvaro," Mrs. Torres said.

Alvaro to came to stand by the bed and took her hand. "Yeah, Mama?"

"I want to wish you good luck today, but you know you can't always count on luck, so do your very best."

"I wish you could be there."

"When you're famous, I'll come and see you perform from the front row."

"I'll hold you to that." Alvaro leaned in to give her a hug. "I love you," he whispered.

"Of course you do. I'm your mama. I love you too, son."

"Let's go," Cande said. "Or I'm going to cry."

"So much drama," Alvaro said lightly as he let go of his mother to put his arm around Cande's shoulders. His eyes sparkled with extra moisture in the light through the window, and Cande was struck by how beautiful his lover was. Pulling his eyes away, he caught Marisol's proud gaze and returned her warm smile of understanding.

"Go on," Alvaro's mother said. "People are waiting for you."

"WHERE have you been?" Eligio said as soon as Alvaro and Cande entered the auditorium. "I called you ages ago."

"Where are Kiki and Leo?" Alvaro asked, ignoring Eligio's fussing.

Eligio jerked a thumb at the stage. Kiki and Leo were dozing, propped back to back in a square of sunlight. "They look like they've been up all night."

"It's a possibility in more than one sense," Alvaro said, making Cande giggle.

Eligio was wound too tight to find humor in anything. "That's not funny," he declared.

"Actually, it is," Cande told him. "If you get the joke. But don't stress. Trust me. You don't want to get this joke."

"You're not making sense," Eligio accused. "And we have a lot of work to do."

"Cande doesn't have to make sense," Alvaro said. "All he has to do is sing and dance and look good at the same time." He bent to shake Kiki's shoulder. "*Oye*! Wake up, *vatos*!"

Leo leapt up, fists balled, blinking in the light. "Alvaro," he said, lowering his hands.

"Who were you expecting?"

"Eligio the Merciless."

Alvaro smiled. "Cande calls him the drill sergeant."

"True that," Kiki said, hooking his fingers in Leo's chinos pocket to haul himself up. "The boy's out of control."

"He's just feeling his power," Cande said. "He'll settle down."

"Or I'll beat him down," Leo said with a dark look in Eligio's direction. "I don't take orders from punks."

"Of course not," Alvaro said. "But you'll work with your friends to be the best we can."

Leo bumped fists with Alvaro. "You got it, bro."

"Then do what Elly says. None of the rest of us gives a crap about organization, but he's good at it. Instead of giving him shit about it, maybe we should thank him."

Kiki laughed. "That was a good one."

"I wasn't kidding," Alvaro said.

"Seriously," Cande put in, "but don't thank him too much. He'll become a monster while trying to please you. He won't know when to stop."

"Well, at least we can stop treating him like a pest," Alvaro persisted.

"I'll be nice," Leo said. "If Eligio will sit in the back seat of the car… and promise not to lick my face or bark at people out the window."

Kiki snickered. "Me too. I'll stop making so much fun of him, but you know there are going to be times when I can't resist. He's just so… decent."

"Are you talking about me?" Eligio called out.

"Yeah, we're discussing what to get you for your birthday," Kiki called back. "Do you already have a Hello Kitty lunchbox?"

Alvaro mock-slapped Kiki's cheek. "Bad Kiki," he said.

"Hey, it was a lot nicer than what I really wanted to say." Kiki's eyebrows disappeared under his bangs. "And I can't help wondering what you're going to say when it finally penetrates Eligio's squeaky clean brain that you and Cande aren't kidding about the sex stuff."

"All right, I guess we shouldn't try to change any habits right now. Let's see if we can nail this routine three times in a row." Alvaro turned to Eligio. "We're ready," he said.

For the next hour, the young men moved across the stage in formation, synching into a smoothly integrated unit. Each step, each gesture, each turn of the head was done in unison, but with the unique flair of the individual. Their movements were powerful but controlled, loose but precise, with a graceful flow that drew the eye irresistibly. Satisfied that the dance steps were second nature, they took a break to eat the sandwiches Eligio had brought. After the early lunch, they practiced singing, running through their vocal parts separately and together until Eligio called a halt, fearing they'd tire their voices. They took another rest to get ready for the final rehearsal, breaking into pairs, leaving Eligio to obsessively go over the festival schedule one more time.

Cande took a deep breath as he stepped out of the building. "Man, they should really invest in some air freshener or something. That auditorium smells like a hundred-year-old jock strap."

"I'll take your word for that." Alvaro followed Cande down the walkway toward the quad, kicking a crushed soda can, juggling it between his feet. When they reached the grassy area, Cande scooped up the can and tossed it into a trash bin.

"It's weird being here on a Saturday," Cande said. "There's no one around."

"It's kind of nice. No lines. You want something?" Alvaro asked, gesturing toward the vending machines.

Cande shook his head as he dropped to the grass. "I just want to be still for a little while."

"No problem." Alvaro lay down on his side next to Cande.

Cande laughed, squinting into the sun. "You haven't been still since I met you, except when you're asleep, and even then you move around a lot. You wake me up about forty times a night."

"Does it bother you?" Alvaro plucked a blade of grass and drew it down the bridge of Cande's nose.

Cande scrunched his nose, rubbing away the tickle with one hand as he batted at Alvaro's hand with the other. "Not really, I like being reminded that I'm not alone. It's worth the bruises."

"We need a bigger bed," Alvaro said, avoiding Cande's hands to run the blade of grass down Cande's neck.

"We'll graduate in a couple of months, and we can take full-time jobs. We'll get a bigger apartment. Your mama needs her own bathroom. She'll cheer up a lot faster if she doesn't have to share with a couple of guys."

"You're very thoughtful." Alvaro tickled the hollow of Cande's throat.

"I hope so. You and Marisol are taking in a virtual stranger, but I'll make sure that you're never sorry you gave me a chance. Cut that out!" Cande grabbed Alvaro's wrist and snatched the stalk of grass from his hand. "It really tickles."

"Yeah, I know. That's why I was doing it. I really like seeing you all stirred up."

"You're such a jerk!" Cande said, but a fond smile belied his words.

Alvaro leaned toward Cande. Just before their lips met, Alvaro's gaze flicked to the right. He sat up and saw Kiki and Leo headed for the vending machines. Cande rose to his elbows, saw their friends, and called out to them. "Why'd you do that?" Alvaro asked reproachfully.

Cande gave him an incredulous look. "You didn't imagine for a second that we were going to get busy right here, did you?"

Alvaro shrugged. "Guess not."

"Don't look so destroyed. Why don't you take all that horny energy and put it into the performance?"

"Are you serious?" Alvaro quickly adjusted himself as Leo and Kiki arrived.

"Serious about what?" Kiki asked as he sat down.

"I was just telling Alvaro that he should cool it and channel all his horniness into his performance."

Leo laughed. "What's the matter, Alvaro? Your boyfriend won't put out?" He feinted a grab at Alvaro's crotch. "Let's see those blue balls."

"I think it's a really good idea," Kiki said. He reached across to slap Cande's palm. "No sex until after the show."

"Hold on," Leo said. "Don't we both have to agree to something like that?"

"Not really," Kiki said. "You can have all the sex you want. Just do it without me."

"I can't win with him," Leo told Cande and Alvaro. "He knows where all my buttons are and just when to push them."

"Then I guess it's a good thing he likes you," Alvaro said. "I like your new necklace, by the way. Yours, too, Kiki."

Kiki smiled. "You know I'm not one to fight against the inevitable."

"What can I say?" Leo shrugged. "He's the one."

"Wow," Cande said. "That's so cool."

"What about the two of you?" Kiki said. "You seem pretty tight."

Cande looked down and then over at Alvaro. Alvaro put a hand on the back of Cande's neck and shook him gently. "Leo said it best. He's the one."

Kiki looked at Cande until Cande met his eyes. "Is that how you feel too?"

Cande nodded, his cheeks turning dark pink. "Now could we talk about something less private?"

"Sorry," Kiki said, squeezing Cande's shoulder. "I'm just looking out for my homie, homie."

"Where the hell are you guys?" Eligio's voice carried clearly across the quad.

"He sounds upset," Cande said.

"Are you kidding?" Kiki said as he stood. "Eligio's so tense today that if he swallowed a charcoal briquette, he'd shit a diamond."

"He needs to chill out," Leo said.

"Then I suggest we all cool it with the public displays of affection in front of him," Cande said. "He seems fairly homophobic. What?" he asked, when the other three burst out laughing.

"Nothing, honeybee," Alvaro said, pulling Cande to his feet.

"Hey!" Cande slapped Alvaro on the upper arm with a loud smack. "You can't call me that. Only Marisol can call me that."

"I don't blame you for wanting to keep it a secret." Alvaro grinned. "Honeybee."

"I hate resorting to tactics like withholding sex, but...." Cande let his words trail off.

"I'm just teasing you and anyway, you're already withholding."

"You can call me honey, if you have to call me anything."

"Okay, honey." Alvaro let go of Cande's hand as Eligio shouted from a closer position. "Poor Elly," he chuckled. "I was worried about him dealing with the fact that I'm gay. Now he'll have Leo and Kiki to deal with too. He's going to feel surrounded by gayness."

"I don't think he's ready," Cande said as they caught up with Leo and Kiki.

"I won't argue with you."

Eligio spotted them and yelled at them to hurry. "Come on. Let's get into our costumes and do a final run-through. And be careful not to get your clothes dirty."

"Give it a rest, Elly," Leo said. "We're not in first year chorus."

"I just want everything to be perfect," Eligio said.

"Well, cut it out," Alvaro said. "Nothing is ever perfect. We're going to do our best, and that's all we can do. Promise me you won't freak out if there's a problem."

"A problem? Why would there be a problem?"

Alvaro clamped a hand around the back of Eligio's neck and looked into his eyes. "Promise me you won't freak out. Because I need you. We all need you. Without you, we're just a bunch of crazy guys running around showing off."

Eligio clenched his jaw and swallowed hard. "I promise," he said.

"Good. I trust you, man." Alvaro clapped his hands. "Why are you standing around? Let's get into our costumes."

Another hour passed in which the boys changed clothes and performed their number in costume. Even Eligio was satisfied with the dress rehearsal and relaxed for a few minutes before he started nagging them to change back into street clothes. They reassembled on the stage with their makeshift costumes tucked into backpacks and gym bags and settled to wait for Mr. Matheson. When half an hour had gone by, Eligio began to look visibly worried.

"He's only ten minutes late," Alvaro said. "And we have hours before we go on stage. We'll get there even if we have to take the bus."

"Mr. Matheson is never late," Eligio said.

"That's not humanly possible," Leo said.

"Who asked you?" Eligio shot back.

"Easy now," Alvaro said. "No freaking out, remember?"

"Why does Leo get to talk disrespectfully about Mr. Matheson?"

"I don't think he meant to be disrespectful," Alvaro said.

Leo shook his head. "I just meant that everyone is late now and then. You can't control things like the weather or traffic accidents."

"Oh. Well, I'm sorry I freaked out," Eligio said. "I'm okay now."

Alvaro patted Eligio's shoulder. "Good man. We're all in this together. If one of us falls out, he takes the rest down with him."

"So… no pressure," Kiki drawled, lightening the mood.

"No pressure at all," Cande spoke up. "You know why?" He looked around the circle. "Because we love this!"

"Yeah!" Leo said loudly. "We love this!"

"And we're damn good at it," Kiki shouted.

"Hell yeah, we are!" Alvaro slapped Kiki's palm.

"We're totally going to kick ass," Eligio said and found himself the focus of four pairs of eyes. "Well, aren't we?"

"Yes we are," Leo said holding up his fist for Eligio to knock.

"All we need is a ride," Alvaro said under his breath. Cande looked up at Alvaro, running a hand down Alvaro's arm. Alvaro glanced aside at Cande and gave him a smile. "We'll get there," Alvaro said.

"I know. I just hope nothing happened to Mr. Matheson. For a teacher, he's not a bad guy."

"He's here!" Eligio exclaimed as one of the lobby doors opened.

"That's not Mr. Matheson," Kiki said.

"Mr. Matheson has car trouble," Mr. Cruz said as he reached the stage. "I would have picked him up, but my car isn't large enough for all of us. Well, what are you waiting for? Pick up your bags and follow me."

"This is a nightmare, right?" Kiki whispered as he picked up his overnight bag.

"I don't care," Alvaro said. "As long as he gets us across town. Come on, guys."

Mr. Cruz opened his trunk, and they loaded the bags inside. Alvaro and Cande sat up front with the teacher while Leo, Kiki, and Eligio squeezed into the back.

"Thank you, sir," Alvaro said as they pulled into traffic. "I don't mean any disrespect, but I'm a little surprised that you're doing us a favor."

"Mr. Matheson called me and said he was in a bind. That's all there is to it. The only reason he called me is that my number was on his answering machine. I guess he doesn't have a lot of friends."

"Maybe not, but he's a good teacher," Cande said softly.

"His students seem to think so," Mr. Cruz said. "I suppose that's worth something. Personally, I'm not sure that music is a suitable subject for a high school. It seems a bit frivolous, and it tends to stir people up."

"A lot of people make careers in music," Alvaro said.

Mr. Cruz sniffed. "I suppose you're right about that. Myself, I don't have a musical bone in my body. I like music, but I don't have a talent for it."

"I'll bet you have some talent, sir," Eligio said, nervously filling the silence. "You just haven't found it yet."

Mr. Cruz cleared his throat, and Eligio sat back between Leo and Kiki. For the rest of the trip it was quiet in the car as the teacher navigated the downtown traffic and brought them safely to the other side. He pulled into the parking lot of a large open-air arena and followed the signs to the performers' entrance. Party of Five presented themselves to the man at the gate, only to be told that they needed their official entry form. Before anyone else could speak, Mr. Cruz volunteered to fetch Mr. Matheson. The gatekeeper pointed Party of Five toward an area just inside the fence. "You can wait over there," he said.

"What next?" Leo wondered gloomily as they leaned against the chain-link fencing.

"A court order from Madonna forbidding us to use her song?" Kiki guessed.

"Why do you have to make a joke out of everything?" Eligio asked. "It must be nice to live in a fancy apartment and never have to worry about money. Maybe everything would be funny to me if I had it so easy."

"Back off," Leo said. "You don't know what you're talking about. At least your family is still together."

Eligio's mouth fell open as he turned to look at Kiki. "I'm sorry," he said. "I didn't know anything had happened to your family."

"Don't worry about it. Lots of people get divorced. I'm sorry if my silliness gets on your nerves." Kiki dropped his gaze. "I used to feel bad most of the time so I made jokes. I guess it's a habit now." He glanced up. "I'll work on it."

"Thanks," Eligio said. "I don't like to admit it, but sometimes you really hurt my feelings."

"I'm sorry," Kiki said again. "Would it help to know that I only tease the people I like?"

Eligio snorted. "You tease everyone."

"Then would it help if I took you for a nice long walk and brushed you?"

Eligio laughed; he couldn't help it. "Throw in a game of fetch and a nice juicy bone?"

Alvaro slapped Eligio on the back. "That's how to handle Kiki, and it didn't hurt a bit, did it?"

Kiki patted Eligio's shoulder. "Plus, it was a good comeback. You have definite potential, Elly."

"I agree." A man's voice broke in. "I was listening to you while I waited for the rest of my equipment to be unloaded. This might sound insensitive, but you're very entertaining."

"Thank you," Alvaro said on a rising note of doubt.

"I won't blame you if you think I'm odd." The round-faced man came closer, taking off his sunglasses and tucking them in one of his many pockets. "I'm Paul Fielder; my company is doing the lighting for the festival."

"We're Party of Five," Alvaro said. "We'll be performing in a few hours."

"*If* Mr. Cruz and Mr. Matheson get back with our entry form," Leo said.

"You're performing 'Lucky Star', right?" Mr. Fielder said. "I noticed that when I was reading the festival schedule. I've never been a big Madonna fan, but I have to admit that she knows how to put on a show. If you boys don't mind some advice: talent is a wonderful thing, but it has to be presented in a way that catches people's attention."

"Good advice," Alvaro said. "Maybe someday we'll have the money for a splashy production."

Mr. Fielder smiled. "Money helps, but you guys have something money can't buy. You're charming. People will want to watch you interact. You should use that. Just a little patter before and after you perform will make your audience feel like they're part of the act."

"So, I guess being a wise-ass could be useful after all." Kiki stroked his chin and wagged his eyebrows.

"That's exactly what I'm talking about," Mr. Fielder said. "It's a wonderful thing to make people laugh."

"I hope we get the chance," Leo said. "We're going to miss our rehearsal time if Mr. Matheson doesn't get here soon."

"Then we'll rehearse right here until they arrive," Alvaro said.

"I like your spirit. I really wish I could help," Mr. Fielder said. "Good luck to you." He bowed and left to supervise the installation of the last minute delivery.

Eligio was devouring his last fingernail when Mr. Matheson came through the gate waving a piece of paper. The young men gathered around the teacher, their relief showing on their faces as they listened to his breathless account of mysterious engine trouble, a desperate appeal to a colleague, and the race back across town. He didn't mention his white-knuckled grip on the dashboard or the near misses with cross-street traffic that turned his knees to jelly. Mr. Cruz had gotten the entry form to the arena on time and saved Party of Five from being disqualified. "I know you won't forget to thank Mr. Cruz," Mr. Matheson said. "He'll join us as soon as he parks the car. We need to report to the backstage area."

Armed with officially stamped papers, Mr. Matheson led the way. He dealt with the backstage organizers and shepherded Party of Five to their designated waiting area. "It's up to you now," he said. "I'll be out front with Mr. Cruz if you need me, but I can't sing or dance for you so you're really on your own."

"I've been on my own for a long time," Cande said. "But not anymore. I feel like I have a family. Even if we don't win tonight, I hope we stay together and try again."

"Of course we will," Alvaro said, putting an arm around Cande's shoulders. "Mr. Fielder is right; when we're together, we're entertainers. We'd be stupid not to give it a shot."

"Mr. Fielder?" Mr. Matheson said. "Not Paul Fielder, by any chance."

"Yeah, that's him," Alvaro said. "He's working the lights."

Mr. Matheson smiled. "I rather doubt it. Mr. Fielder owns the theatrical supply company that donates the lighting to the festival every year, along with most of the sound equipment. He was a promoter years ago, but I guess there's more money in the rental business. At any rate, he's seen the best, so if he gave you a compliment, you should be proud."

"Huh," Leo said, "he didn't look rich."

"Not everyone likes to advertise their wealth," the music teacher said. "Now I'll say good luck and go rescue Mr. Cruz from the fascists who call themselves the festival committee." He paused. "Perhaps you shouldn't repeat my last remark. It was... injudicious."

"Don't worry, Mr. Matheson," Alvaro said. "Everyone's injudicious once in a while. Thank you for all your help." The rest of the boys echoed Alvaro's thanks as Mr. Matheson left. Alvaro looked down at Cande. "What's injudicious?" he whispered.

"You're injudicious," Cande replied as an organizer stopped by to tell them to move up to the boys' dressing room area. Behind fabric screens set up for the occasion, they changed from street clothes to their makeshift costumes.

"Not bad," Kiki said as he surveyed his band mates. Each was wearing a school uniform that had been modified with no regard for its later use. Leo had ripped the sleeves off his jacket and wore a red tank top underneath. Alvaro had done away with his shirt and jacket and was wearing a red vest and tie over his bare chest. Eligio's uniform was nearly intact but he wore jeans like the rest and a pair of high top sneakers that had been dyed bright red. Kiki was shirtless, his jacket unbuttoned and his sleeves pushed up, a red fedora cocked rakishly over one eye. Cande wore his white button-down shirt open to the waist with a long red scarf around his hips like a sash. Like their singing voices and dancing styles, each outfit was unique, but complemented the others. The touches of red, the glittering chains hanging from their necks, belt loops and boots, and their excited smiles attracted attention and several heads turned to watch as Party of Five left the changing area.

"All set?" An organizer wearing a headset guided the band to a spot next to the steps to the stage. "You'll be rehearsing next. You have fifteen minutes to coordinate the lights and music with your act, and then you'll exit on the opposite side. Someone will be there to tell you where to go next."

"Thank you," Alvaro said. When the official left to fetch the next group, Alvaro turned to his friends. "This is our only chance to make changes and requests, so let's not waste it. Instead of everyone making suggestions, I think Kiki and Cande should speak for us. Agreed?"

When they got onstage, they ran through their routine to the recorded music while a programmed sequence of lights flashed on and off. As the last note faded, a voice came through the sound system. "Hello again! It's Mr. Fielder here. Glad to see you made it. Listen, my lighting guy has a great program he put together for a Madonna tribute. Would you like to see some of the 'Lucky Star' sequence?"

Kiki glanced at Alvaro. If they didn't like the light show, they'd have wasted half of their rehearsal time. On the other hand, Mr. Fielder was a professional. "What do you say, Alvaro?"

"We started this together," Alvaro said. "What do *you* say?"

"I think we should listen to a professional."

"Done," Alvaro said. "Thank you, Mr. Fielder," he called out. "We'd like to see the program."

"Whenever you're ready," Mr. Fielder said. The members of Party of Five got into position. The light man signaled to the sound operator, and the music started. The group went into their routine and performed it without a hitch. When they froze in the last of several static poses, they realized that everyone had stopped what they were doing to watch. "Wonderful!" Mr. Fielder said into his microphone. "You're welcome to use the program unless it's against the rules."

"Thank you," Alvaro said as an organizer gestured from the other side of the stage. Party of Five was directed to yet another waiting area where they stood around and tried not to be nervous. There were a lot of acts ahead of them ranging from good to very good to a couple that were stars in the making. It wasn't difficult to see who the main competition was.

"Damn, they were really good," Leo said as a six-girl singing group left the stage.

Kiki nodded. "I had tears in my eyes when the little one hit those high notes. She was adorable and a hell of a good singer."

"Between them and that dancing acrobatic group...." Alvaro's voice trailed off as he glanced at Cande.

"The Klown Kings," Cande supplied the name of the group.

"Right, the Klown Kings," Alvaro said. "Them... and the Snow Whites that just sang are the ones to beat."

"We can do it," Eligio said. "I know we can, if we all just concentrate."

Alvaro moved to stand with his shoulder touching Eligio's. "We're all going to give it everything we've got," he said, as he pulled Cande to stand at his other shoulder. Leo and Kiki moved in to close the circle, shutting out the noise and activity around them. "This group has gone through a lot of changes in a short time," Alvaro said. "It started out as joke between me and Kiki. We were always doing dance routines together, and we made a pact that we'd be stars some day. At some point, Leo stopped making fun of us and joined us. People laughed at us but we kept practicing whenever we had time. We were good enough last year to be accepted for the competition."

"My arrest for shoplifting kind of fucked that up," Kiki said.

"That's the past," Alvaro said. "Right now, we're dealing with the present. All of us need to be as present as we can. Make each second count. Don't let up your intensity until we walk off the stage. I know I can do it. Will each of you promise me the same?"

"You got it, man," Leo said instantly.

"I'll be as serious as first-degree murder," Kiki said.

Eligio nodded solemnly.

Cande met Alvaro's eyes. "I won't let you down."

"Then we can't lose," Alvaro said. "Deep breaths, everyone. Here comes an official."

The event staffer gestured to Party of Five to follow and led them to a carpeted area beside the steps. The band members clasped hands one last time and then applauded as the previous act left the stage. Their names were announced. They picked up their microphones, and then they were moving, bouncing up the stairs and into the lights in front of the thousand or so festivalgoers that made up the record-breaking crowd. Surprised by number of people, Eligio slowed his step and Leo bumped into him, making him stumble.

"Have a nice trip?" Kiki said without thinking, his microphone picking up the words and amplifying them. The audience laughed, the sound growing louder as more people joined in.

"It was a nice trip," Eligio replied when the laughter died down. "I hope I'll see you next fall." He grinned as the schoolyard retort got the crowd laughing again.

"I've already fallen for you." Kiki couldn't resist the comeback. He clasped his hands under his chin and batted his eyelashes as he leaned toward Eligio.

Eligio recoiled. "Thanks, but no thanks."

Alvaro raised his microphone and cleared his throat. "Hey, guys? We're here to sing a song, remember?"

Kiki and Eligio turned toward Alvaro in exaggerated surprise as the audience continued to laugh. After bowing low to Alvaro, Kiki, and Eligio faced the crowd and struck the sort of poses usually seen in heroic statues. Alvaro put his hand on his hip and tapped his foot until Cande and Leo imitated Kiki and Eligio. Hoisting his fist skyward as though holding an invisible sword, Alvaro glanced into the wings and nodded. The anxious technician running the sound board pushed a button, and the lighting supervisor flipped a switch. Sound and color enveloped the stage, and Party of Five moved with the music and the light, their voices and bodies melding smoothly with the rhythm, the flash, and the heat. The combination of their flawless harmonies and their athletic bodies moving with power and grace won over an audience that had already been wooed by their effortless charm. When the performance ended, the applause was loud and sustained. Party of Five took a bow and trotted off as they'd been instructed in rehearsal. At the bottom of the stairs, an organizer waved them back. After a moment of confusion, the band returned to the stage and bowed again as the applause continued. As one, Party of Five thanked the crowd and left the stage.

"Holy shit!" Leo panted, bending to rest his hands on his knees. Kiki leaned limply against a pole as he got his breath back. Alvaro hugged Cande tight, their chests heaving for air, mile-wide grins on their faces. Eligio sank into a squat, elbows on his thighs, hands hanging between his knees. "We did it," he breathed.

A staffer came with towels, and the young men gratefully mopped the sweat from their faces. They were told not to leave the area and that someone would call for them when the judging was over. Realizing this meant they were finalists, they celebrated with hugs and a few jiggy dance steps, their exhaustion abruptly forgotten in the rush of adrenaline.

"Oh man, it's really real," Eligio said. "We could really win this thing."

Leo thumbed tears off Kiki's cheeks. "You feel better now about letting us down last year, clown?"

Kiki nodded, no longer able to trust his voice. Leo put an arm around Kiki and pulled him into a hug. Kiki buried his face in his lover's shoulder as the tears continued to come. Leo started to speak, but his throat tightened, and in another moment, he was crying too. "Hey, come on," Alvaro said. "Save it for when we actually win." Leo flapped a hand at Alvaro to mind his own business. Alvaro turned away and saw tears trembling in Cande's eyes. "Not you too." Alvaro shook his head. "Don't you start, Eligio, or I'll break." Eligio snorted at the very idea of becoming emotional, but his throat had closed up, and he was glad his reply was interrupted by the return of a festival representative.

Alvaro's earlier prediction proved good, and Party of Five found themselves on stage with the Klown Kings and the Snow Whites. The performers were judged by a panel of professionals and by audience response as the master of ceremonies invited the crowd to applaud for each of the three acts in turn. For a few minutes that felt like eternity, the judges deliberated before handing the results to the emcee. The host read the name of the third place winner, and the Klown Kings did their best to look pleased. Second place went to Party of Five, leaving the Snow Whites to take top honors. Though disappointed, the boys knew that second prize was a real triumph, and Mr. Matheson's reaction cheered them up. The sight of a teacher jumping up and down with joy put smiles on all their faces.

"You were the best," Mr. Cruz said, shaking hands with each of the young men. "You should have won, but I heard the judges saying that you were too… sexy."

"I told you we should tone that stuff down," Eligio said.

"We did," Kiki answered.

"I wasn't trying to dance sexy," Cande protested.

Mr. Matheson laughed. "Dancing is innately sexy, and there's nothing wrong with that. It's the judges who are narrow-minded, or short-sighted, take your pick."

"You still get a very nice cash prize." Mr. Cruz coughed. "Mr. Matheson and I would like to buy dinner for you as a celebration."

"Thank you." Alvaro bowed. "Just let us change out of our costumes."

When the young men returned in street clothes, Mr. Cruz and Mr. Matheson had been joined by Mr. Fielder and another man. "Gentlemen!" Mr. Matheson called out. "Come and meet Mr. Fielder's friend. He wants to congratulate you."

"This is Mr. Roman Beckermann," Mr. Fielder said. "We worked together a long time ago before we both decided to quit show business." He smiled. "Of course, I didn't go far away."

"Let me talk," Mr. Beckermann said. "You have a way of making short stories long. Boys, I'm an agent who used to be a manager. I don't do much of either anymore, but I'm damned if I'm going to let an opportunity like this go by."

"What kind of opportunity?" Alvaro asked.

"I've never seen a band with as much raw potential as you have. Talent scouts dream of finding performers like you. I'm sure a couple of guys that I saw in the audience will be contacting you tomorrow or the next day, but thanks to my friend Mr. Fielder, I'm here now with my foot in the door, so to speak. There's only one thing I can offer you that they can't; I won't screw you."

"He's an honest guy," Mr. Fielder said. "If he says he won't screw you, then he won't."

"There are a lot of unscrupulous types in the entertainment business," Mr. Beckermann said. "That's why Mr. Fielder retired. If you want to keep your self-respect, it's hard to work in show business sometimes. But I'm willing to give it a try again."

"What kind of capital do you have?" Eligio asked.

Mr. Matheson gasped, but Mr. Beckermann chuckled. "I'm not offended; it's a smart question. You can come and stand by me, young man. As for capital, I have enough funds for a good start, and Mr. Fielder is interested in investing in you also."

"Could we get any luckier?" Alvaro wondered aloud.

"It's more likely that your hard work is being rewarded." Mr. Cruz said.

"I don't care which it is," Leo said. "Just nobody pinch me. If I'm dreaming, I want to stay asleep. Ow!" He yelped and rubbed his butt. Kiki looked innocently up at the night sky as his lips puckered in a whistle.

"Mr. Matheson and Mr. Cruz have kindly asked me to join you for dinner," Mr. Beckermann said. "This will give me a chance to pick up the check and win Mr. Domingo's heart."

"What?" Eligio said as his friends laughed. "What's so funny?"

"Never mind," Mr. Beckermann said. "You have a real head for business. Never undervalue it."

"Shall we go, then?" Mr. Matheson said. "I know it's Saturday night, but it is getting late."

"I'm a little worried about leaving my mother alone for so long," Alvaro said when they reached the parking lot.

"Call her," Cande said.

Alvaro looked startled, as though it had never occurred to him to phone his mother. "Okay, as soon as we find—" He broke off as Kiki thrust a cell phone into his hand. "I'll call her now."

While Alvaro made his call, Mr. Beckermann led Mr. Matheson, Kiki, and Leo to his car. Alvaro's mother answered and told him not to dare come home, that he should be celebrating with his friends, having a good time. "I'll try, Mama," he said, his gaze going to Cande. "Good night." By the time Alvaro hung up, Cande had climbed into the back seat with Eligio, leaving the front seat open. Alvaro got in, glancing into the rear of the car before he faced front and fastened his seat belt.

He was happy they'd taken second place at the Spring Festival. He was ecstatic that a bona fide agent was interested in Party of Five. But the promises he'd just seen in Cande's eyes put him over the moon. He knew in that moment that no matter what other miracles came to pass, he'd never forget this night for the rest of his life, and it wasn't over yet.

chapter Ten

JUST after midnight, Mr. Cruz dropped the boys off at the school. He was willing to take them to their doorsteps, but they protested that he'd already gone to too much trouble for them. "Congratulations again," the teacher said as he drove away.

"Anyone want to do anything?" Leo asked.

Eligio shook his head. "I told Mama and Papa not to wait up, but I know them. I'd better go home so they can go to bed. They have to be up so early."

"It's no picnic running your own business," Leo said.

"I help out as much as I can," Eligio said immediately.

"Don't get so defensive," Leo said. "I was just trying to compliment your family for being hard workers."

"Oh." Eligio floundered for a reply. "Thanks," he said at last. "Are we going to meet up tomorrow?"

"I'm planning to sleep in a little," Alvaro said. "But I'd like to get together with everyone sometime tomorrow."

"Why don't you all come to my house?" Eligio said. "I know my folks will want to congratulate you."

"I thought your mama said we were a bad influence," Kiki said.

"She sounds like a smart woman," Cande said.

"Just come by in the afternoon," Eligio said. "I think maybe my parents planned a little party or something in case we won." He finished unchaining his bicycle and climbed on. "So, are you all coming by tomorrow?" After receiving four affirmatives, he rode away.

"He thinks that *maybe* his parents planned something?" Kiki said when Eligio was out of earshot. "What do you want to bet that there's a party with a cake and everything?"

"I'll bet you're right," Leo said.

"We should wear something nice," Alvaro said. "I just hope I have a clean shirt. I haven't done laundry in days."

"Listen to us," Cande said. "We've just had the most exciting night our lives, and we're talking about laundry."

"Not all of us, just Alvaro," Kiki said. "He's obsessed with housework; didn't you know?"

"I've never seen any evidence of that," Cande said.

Kiki and Leo laughed, leaning against one another. Alvaro gave Cande a reproachful look. "Are you saying I'm a slob?" he asked.

"Of course not," Cande patted Alvaro's cheek. "I'd never use a word like slob. You are a bit of a pig, though."

"No comeback?" Kiki asked when it became obvious that Alvaro wasn't going to reply.

Alvaro shook his head. "I have nothing bad to say about Cande."

The impish smiled melted from Cande's face as he moved closer to Alvaro. Putting his hands on Alvaro's shoulders, he brought their lips together. Ignoring the whistles and hoots from their friends, Cande kissed Alvaro sweetly and thoroughly. Alvaro's hands settled on Cande's hips as he responded, kissing Cande's nose, forehead, chin, cheeks, and ears before returning to his mouth.

"Aren't they sweet?" Leo remarked.

"They're inspiring," Kiki answered, slipping an arm around Leo's waist.

Alvaro broke the kiss to look at his friends. "Go find some other porn to watch."

"Aw, come on," Kiki said. "You were just getting to the good part."

Alvaro grinned. "Not even close. Look, I know I'm a stallion and Cande is a wet dream come true, but you can't watch."

Leo shrugged. "We're way hotter than you guys anyway."

"No one's hotter than my honey," Alvaro said.

"I'm changing the subject," Kiki said. "What time do you want to meet up tomorrow?"

"Why don't we wait for Eligio to call and tell us?" Alvaro said.

"Fine," Leo said. "Ready to go home and have our own private celebration?" he asked Kiki, wrapping his arms around his lover from behind.

Kiki gave Alvaro and Cande an apologetic look. "He wants me," he said with a shrug.

Alvaro looked at his friend in the arms of another friend, meeting Kiki's happy gaze. Several complicated emotions were communicated in a heartbeat, and both young men smiled. "He looks good on you," Alvaro said softly.

Kiki held out his arms. Alvaro stepped into the hug, wrapping his arms around Kiki and Leo. After the briefest hesitation, Cande joined the group embrace, putting an arm around Alvaro's back and one around Leo's.

"Eligio should be here," Cande said.

"This is too much guy-touching for him," Kiki said. "He'd be scarred for life."

"It's not like we're having an orgy," Cande protested.

"We're having an orgy?" Leo repeated with exaggerated excitement.

Alvaro smacked the back of Leo's head, and the hug broke up. "Good night," Alvaro said to Kiki and Leo. He took Cande's hand and walked away from the school. Behind them, they heard Leo's motorcycle start up, and a couple of minutes later, Leo and Kiki roared past them with a wave. Alvaro and Cande waved back as the bike sped away.

"Take me home and take me to bed," Kiki said in Leo's ear. Leo nodded and opened the throttle a little more. Kiki held on to his lover as the lights became bright smears in his peripheral vision, and the wind of their passage roared in his ears. The exhilarating speed and anticipation of making love had Kiki vibrating with excitement by the time Leo parked the bike. Whipping off his helmet, Kiki grabbed Leo and kissed him hard.

"Whoa!" Leo breathed when their lips parted. Taking Kiki's hand, he pulled him to a darker area of the parking lot. As soon as they were out of the light, he wrapped his arms around Kiki and took his mouth with a passion that left Kiki breathless.

"This thing isn't cooling off one little bit," Kiki said softly.

Leo shook his head. "I want you so much I can't believe it. When I used to imagine my future, I never thought I'd fall in love with a guy."

"I thought I was in love with Alvaro for a long time."

"What?" Leo snickered. "You're kidding."

"I guess I hid it well, huh?"

"I never would've suspected. You're such a ladies' man. I always envied the way you picked up chicks so easy." He laughed again. "That's kind of—"

"Ironic?"

"Yeah. Enough talk," Leo said, covering Kiki's mouth with his again. He slid his hands down Kiki's shoulders and upper arms, moving to grip Kiki's slim hips to pull him closer. Kiki took control of the kiss, thrusting deep into Leo's mouth, fingertips massaging Leo's scalp. Leo moaned as his mouth was plundered, his fingers sinking into the muscles of Kiki's ass, kneading and parting the firm cheeks. A soft growl rose from Kiki's chest as Leo sucked at his tongue. He backed Leo up against the bulk of an anonymous SUV and pumped his hips, rubbing their crotches together. "Oh man, that is sweet, sweet, sweet,"

Leo murmured as Kiki nuzzled his ear, tongue tracing the whorls, nibbling at the lobe. A sudden light dazzled Leo's eyes.

"What are you punks up to?" asked the man with the flashlight.

Kiki let go of Leo and took step away from the vehicle. "I live here," he said. The parking lot attendant shone his light in Kiki's face, and Kiki put a hand up to shade his eyes. "Do I look familiar?" he said sarcastically.

"What's your name?"

"Enrique Viera. I'm in 14A."

The attendant lowered the flashlight. "Sorry, but some vandals have broken into a couple of cars in the neighborhood, and the two of you looked suspicious."

Leo frowned, and Kiki spoke quickly. "Well, we're not. Good night and keep up the good work." Kiki gestured for Leo to follow him as he walked away.

"What a jerk," Leo said, glancing over his shoulder.

"He's just doing his job," Kiki said as they walked into the building.

"Well, his timing sucks." Leo pushed Kiki into the elevator ahead of him and pressed him to the wall. Kiki returned the passionate kiss, taking Leo by the upper arms and flipping him so his back was to the wall. Leo grinned into the kiss, and they spent the remainder of the ride vying for dominance and snickering like fourth graders. When the doors opened, they broke apart, straightened their faces, and nodded courteously to the couple waiting to get on the elevator. Mr. and Mrs. Young's disapproving expressions made Leo and Kiki burst into laughter again as they practically sprinted down the hall.

Kiki opened the apartment door and was flung to the carpet when Leo tackled him from behind. "The door," Kiki gasped as Leo let him up for air. "Close the fucking door."

Leo kicked backward and the door slammed shut. "Happy now?"

"Delirious." Kiki grabbed Leo's shoulders and rolled on top of him. Looking down into his lover's gleaming eyes, he slowly licked his lips. "You look very tasty. I think I'll eat you."

"Not if I eat you first."

Kiki's rich chuckle rubbed sensuously against Leo's ears and vibrated in his groin. "No reason we can't both get what we want," he said. Leo shivered as Kiki licked the sensitive spot behind his earlobe. Kiki smiled as he kissed and nibbled his way downward, unbuttoning Leo's shirt and unzipping his pants on the way. Leo moved restlessly, his hands groping at random bits of Kiki until he got hold of Kiki's hard-on. Kiki sucked in a sharp breath as Leo squeezed firmly. "Hang on," Kiki said. He unfastened his pants and peeled them down, toeing off his sneakers in the process. Turning so that he faced Leo's feet, he pulled Leo's arousal through the fly of his jeans. He'd planned on teasing his lover a little, but as soon as he saw Leo's cock, he had to taste it.

"Oh fuck!" Leo gasped as the head of his shaft was surrounded by hot wet velvet. He held his breath as Kiki engulfed his full length. Grabbing onto Kiki's hips, Leo pulled his lover down until he could get his mouth on Kiki's cock. He found Kiki's balls first and got distracted as he tongued and sucked at the hanging weight, breathing deeply of the earthy scent. Kiki wrapped his arms around Leo's muscular thighs and bobbed his head, lips sliding up and down Leo's spit-shiny shaft. Leo's hand slid up to rest on the small of Kiki's back, pressing down, bringing Kiki's crotch in closer contact with his face. Kiki took the hint, rocking gently as Leo's tongue ran the length of his cock over and over. "Let's change position a little," Leo murmured, his lips teasing Kiki's foreskin.

Kiki took his mouth off Leo's cock as Leo tipped them onto their sides. With a delighted smile, Leo sucked in the head of Kiki's shaft and swirled his tongue around it. Kiki's eyes drifted shut in ecstasy as he burrowed into Leo's crotch again, and the race was on between two naturally competitive young men. Licking, sucking, stroking, probing, each did his best to make his lover come first in a healthy and highly pleasurable contest that had no real loser. Leo felt the inevitable wind-up of his climax and prodded Kiki's armpit with his toes. Kiki laughed, or tried to with a mouth full of Leo, and broke his rhythm. When Kiki felt his balls tighten, he pictured Eligio walking in on them and he was able to stave off his orgasm. Leo spit on his index finger and eased it into Kiki. "So that's how you want to play," Kiki groaned as Leo found his prostate. Kiki worked a finger into Leo and found the slight swelling that made Leo moan. They'd only recently discovered this pleasure, and it didn't take long before both were at the point of no return. Lips stretched wide, nostrils flared in the fight for breath, they rocked against each other, thrusting and sucking, swallowing and shuddering as they came.

"Fuck," Leo breathed as he pulled his mouth from Kiki's spent rod. "That was the best ever. The best!"

"No argument." Kiki rested his cheek against Leo's flat belly. "What a night!"

Leo stared up at the ceiling as afterglow began to steal through him cell by cell. "It's freaky how your life can change so fast."

"True that." Kiki puckered his lips and blew a cool stream of air over Leo's cock.

Leo reached down and pulled Kiki up into his arms. Kiki settled against Leo's chest, idly toying with a caramel-kiss nipple. They were quiet for several minutes, content to hold one another and let the aftereffects of great sex sink in.

"Do you really think we'll be rich and famous some day?" Leo broke the silence.

"I'd prefer to be rich and obscure," Kiki said.

"Be serious for a minute."

"Yeah, I think we probably have a better than average chance of being a hit band if we get a few more breaks and keep working our asses off."

Leo hugged Kiki tight. "That's what I think too."

"Is that what you want?"

"Huh? How can you ask me that? Think of what I could do with the money. My brother wouldn't have to worry about where his tuition was coming from. He wouldn't have to wait tables to buy books. Maybe my mom and my pops could even quit working."

"Are you going to spend any of it on yourself?"

"I'll probably trick my bike out."

Kiki chuckled softly. "I love you, Leo Lazaro."

"I love you twice as much," Leo answered immediately.

"I love you times infinity." Kiki gave his lover a gloating smile.

"I love you as much as Alvaro loves Cande."

"Damn!" Kiki reacted to being bested. "I thought I had you when I said times infinity because, face it, what's more than infinity? It's like saying more perfect. Perfect is perfect, you know? You can't improve on it."

"Like my blow job?"

Kiki chuckled. "No. Like *my* blow job."

"It was really good," Leo conceded.

"Yours too." Kiki sat up. "Want to go to bed?"

"I notice you didn't ask if I wanted to go to sleep."

"I love you for your brain," Kiki said, pulling Leo to his feet.

Leo put his cock away and slipped an arm around Kiki's waist. "Do you think Alvaro and Cande are doing the same thing right now?"

"I hope so. At least I hope they aren't wondering what we're doing," Kiki teased as he pulled away and darted into the bedroom with Leo close behind.

"THIS is where we had our first kiss," Cande said as they reached the walkway over the tracks. He stopped and leaned on the railing.

"No it isn't," Alvaro said. "The first time I kissed you was on the roof."

"Are you sure?"

"Of course, I am. I'll never forget it."

"Okay." Cande conceded, gazing down the tracks.

"You really don't remember?"

"I got mixed up."

"Or it didn't mean as much to you as it did to me."

"Maybe it didn't at the time. Are we about to have a fight?"

Alvaro swallowed the first words that sprang to his lips and thought for a minute before he spoke. "No, we're not going to fight. Not about this. Just because I wanted you the second I saw you doesn't mean you have to feel the same way. We're different people, that's all."

"I wanted you the second I saw you," Cande said. "But this isn't about wanting. I don't fall in love as easily as you do." He paused. "I don't mean that you're easy; it just takes me a while to trust people."

"You trust me now, right?"

Cande nodded.

"And you love me."

Cande nodded again.

"I'll try not to be too hurt when you forget our anniversary," Alvaro said.

Cande giggled and turned to take Alvaro in his arms. "You'll remind me," he said. "And I think my memory will start improving when I have some good things to remember."

"I'm going to give you all kinds of good things to remember," Alvaro promised. "So many that you won't have room for the bad memories."

"I like your plan for the future." Cande looked up into Alvaro's eyes. "Come on. Let's go somewhere else and make out like crazy."

"I like *your* plan for the future." Alvaro gave Cande a quick kiss before his lover pulled away from him with a laugh. Then he was chasing Cande down the sidewalk, around parked cars and streetlights until they reached the park. Cande dashed between the hedges and onto the playground. Alvaro caught up with him at the slide, dodging back and forth until Cande climbed the ladder to stand at the top. Laughing breathlessly, Cande came down the slide to crash into Alvaro. Alvaro went over backward, landing with Cande on top of him. Cande took the opportunity for revenge, deploying a sneak tickle attack. "Help!" Alvaro gasped between chuckles. "I'm being molested."

"You're getting what you richly deserve," Cande said, as Alvaro bucked and shook beneath him. "Beg for mercy."

Alvaro was so convulsed with laughter that he could barely breathe. "Please," he wheezed.

Cande let up. "And don't even think about getting me back. If your fingers go anywhere near my ticklish spots, you'll lose all access."

Alvaro blinked away the extra moisture in his eyes and met Cande's gaze. "We're even for now," he said, and then he drew a deep breath. "I'm as limp as a boiled noodle. You could do anything to me right now, and I'd be helpless to stop you."

"Anything?" Cande let all of his weight rest on Alvaro.

"Almost anything," Alvaro amended.

"So there are limits to your love," Cande said playfully.

"There's nothing I wouldn't do for you," Alvaro said. "But there are a few things I'd rather not do."

"Should we make a list?"

"I'd rather kiss you." Alvaro rolled so that Cande was on the bottom. He leaned in and pressed his lips to Cande's, moving them gently until Cande's mouth opened. In little teasing darts of his tongue, Alvaro licked Cande's lips and the interior of his mouth. Cande returned the enticing caress, his tongue sliding against Alvaro's as his hands slid down Alvaro's back. Grabbing Alvaro's ass, Cande pulled him closer as the kiss grew hotter and sloppier. "*Aiy*," Alvaro groaned as Cande nibbled at his chin. "We need to go somewhere more private."

"But you like doing it outside."

"We're right out in the open. Anyone walking by could see us."

"It's the middle of the night." Cande pouted as Alvaro got to his feet. He took the hand Alvaro offered him, but turned aside from a kiss. "I was really enjoying that," he said.

"We can take up where we left off in just a couple of minutes."

"Really? What did you have in mind? Because it's more than a couple of minutes to your place."

"Would I make you wait?"

Cande raised his eyebrows. "What are you doing right now if you're not making me wait?"

"You're really turned on, huh?"

"Getting less so by the second."

"Come on." Alvaro took Cande's hand again. "Trust me."

"Where are we?" Cande asked as he followed Alvaro down several alleys and finally, through a broken out window.

Alvaro turned to catch Cande in his arms. "In a warehouse."

Cande stuck out his tongue. "Duh."

"It's just used for storage. No one's moved a thing in here for years. It used to be our clubhouse," Alvaro said as he led Cande across the floor. "Me and Leo and Kiki and a few other guys used to surf every day in the summer. Mostly we hung out on the beach, but when the weather was bad, we came here." Alvaro opened a door on a small room. "This used to be an office. Most of the furniture was here but we added more from the junkyard."

Cande eyed the heap of blankets in the corner. "Is there a mattress under there?"

"Absolutely, and it's been well tested."

"By you?"

"By a lot of people, but yeah, I've gotten some action here."

Cande put a hand on Alvaro's chest. "I wish I could have learned about sex with you."

Alvaro heard years of unspoken pain in Cande's voice. He put his hand over his lover's as he swallowed hard. "Me too."

"I don't want to be jealous of the ones who got to kiss you and hold you before me. I don't like feeling jealous at all, but when it comes to you, everything is different."

"That proves you love me," Alvaro said. "Personally, I can't stand the thought of you with anyone but me."

"Varo," Cande said softly before Alvaro's lips could touch his.

"What?" Alvaro's breath was warm on Cande's cheek, as sweet and intoxicating as the rum and Coke they'd had with dinner.

"I have to say this. I want to be with you, and I want to be good, but my past... I just don't have a good track record. I'm afraid—"

"Don't be," Alvaro interrupted. "There's nothing wrong with you, Cande Carlisle. You just had some bad things happen to you, and I'm here now to protect you."

"I'm afraid I'll hurt *you*," Cande finished his sentence.

"Maybe you will. Maybe I'll hurt you. Who knows? Let's just do our best not to hurt one another, okay?"

"And that's enough for you? My promise that I'll try not to hurt you?"

"What more can I ask?"

Cande grabbed a handful of Alvaro's hair and yanked him into a wet collision of lips, teeth, and tongues. Alvaro wasn't slow to respond, pulling Cande even closer as the kiss grew deeper. Cande worked the tail of Alvaro's shirt from the back of his jeans and slid a hand up his lover's spine. Alvaro moaned as Cande's fingertips sank into the muscles of his back, stroking and kneading. Cande's grip on Alvaro's hair was painful, but it barely registered amid the welter of sensations. Each urgent touch, each slide of lip over lip, each soft sigh added another degree to the feverish excitement that was growing hotter by the second. Alvaro took hold of Cande's ass and pressed their crotches together as he kissed a fiery trail down the curve of Cande's throat. Cande took hold of Alvaro's head with both hands, fingers weaving into the thick hair as Alvaro's teeth closed on his left nipple. Alvaro nibbled the small nub to hardness and then sucked at it, soaking the cotton of Cande's shirt. Cande moaned at the exquisite friction of the fabric rubbing against his nipple as Alvaro licked at it. Alvaro worked a hand between them to squeeze Cande's crotch as he moved his mouth to Cande's right nipple. "Varo," Cande groaned as Alvaro's free hand toyed with his abandoned left nipple.

"What is it?" Alvaro mumbled, plucking at Cande's shirt with his teeth.

"Can we sit down?"

A proud smile lit Alvaro's face. "Am I getting to you?"

"I never knew how much I liked this stuff," Cande said breathlessly. "I thought I was pretty experienced, but quantity is obviously no substitute for quality."

Alvaro ignored the sting of the implication that Cande had been with a lot of people. After all, Alvaro had done his share of playing the field. "That almost sounded like a compliment."

"It's a compliment," Cande answered as Alvaro steered him to the desk a few steps behind him. "You're a stud."

"I don't want to be a stud." Alvaro chuckled. "Okay, that's a lie. I do want to be a stud, but I want to be your stud." Putting his hands on Cande's pliant waist, Alvaro helped him up to sit on the edge of the desk.

Cande laughed softly. "Tough guy," he said. "So cute." He kissed the end of Alvaro's nose.

Alvaro moved between Cande's thighs and unbuttoned Cande's shirt. Yanking the shirt down Cande's arms, Alvaro leaned in to capture one of Cande's nipples with his mouth. Slowly, he drew the tip of his tongue around it. "Still think I'm cute?" he murmured.

"I'll think whatever you want if you keep doing that." Cande leaned back on the palms of his hands and looked at Alvaro with heavy-lidded eyes. "You're driving me crazy."

Alvaro leaned over Cande, bringing their hard-ons into close contact. He shifted his weight, and Cande moaned as their cocks were mashed together. Alvaro licked at Cande's nipples, wanting to hear that needy noise again. To the primal accompaniment of Cande's groans, sighs and whimpers, Alvaro played his lover like a favorite melody. Cande was responsive to a degree that approached violent, and Alvaro loved it. Each tug at his hair, every bruisingly strong grip was a sincere tribute to his effect on his lover. There was no more of the holding back that Cande had done the first few times they were together. "I love you so much," Alvaro said as he worked the zipper of his boyfriend's jeans. Cande gasped as Alvaro took hold of his cock and tried to swallow it. In seconds, Cande's cum was hitting the back of Alvaro's throat. Alvaro drank it down and relinquished the sated shaft to kiss his way back up his lover's trembling body. Cande tasted the vaguely salty dregs of his essence as Alvaro's tongue thrust into his mouth and an achingly strong pulse of desire tightened his groin.

"Come up here," Cande said as he broke the kiss.

Alvaro climbed up to kneel on the desk straddling Cande. Cande unfastened Alvaro's jeans and peeled them down until he freed Alvaro's leaking cock. Wrapping his arms around Alvaro's thighs, Cande buried his face in Alvaro's crotch, kissing and licking. He sucked each of Alvaro's balls into his mouth, rolling them around until Alvaro groaned in ecstasy. Leaving the velvety sack, Cande lapped and sucked at Alvaro's shaft like it was the best hard candy he'd ever tasted. Alvaro threw his head back, panting with pleasure as Cande lavished attention on his arousal. He was more than a little disappointed when the caresses stopped. "What?" he said a bit groggily. "Is something wrong?"

Cande was wriggling against the wood as he tried to get his jeans all the way off. He was stymied by his shoes, which were now wedged in his pants legs. "Help me," he said.

Alvaro didn't argue, but he was a little puzzled. "I was kind of liking the blow job," he said.

"I thought you might want to take it to the next level," Cande answered.

"What do you mean?" Alvaro asked as he managed to get Cande's jeans all the way off.

Cande whipped off his underwear and shirt and smiled up at Alvaro. "You can guess, can't you?" he said, as he leaned back on his elbows and let his legs sprawl wide.

"Oh man," Alvaro breathed. Even in the dim light, Cande's skin shone like the inside of a shell. "I can't believe how beautiful you are."

"What are you waiting for?" Cande sounded a little upset that Alvaro hadn't moved.

"I want to do it. I really do, but…." Alvaro's voice trailed off.

"But what? I'm offering myself to you and you're just standing there."

"Hey," Alvaro said softly. "Don't be mad. I want you more than I've ever wanted anything in my life. I just don't want to do it here like this."

"Like what?"

"In a hurry… on an old piece of office furniture." Alvaro paused. "Without any lubricant."

"I don't care about that stuff. I want you." Cande held out his arms. "I want you inside me."

"You're killing me," Alvaro said. "But even if you do get mad at me, I want to wait."

"You feel strongly about this, huh?"

"Yeah, I do. The few times I've gone all the way were with girls. I don't know how to make love to a guy and not for anything will I take a chance on hurting you."

"Come here," Cande said, scooting back to the edge of the desk and taking Alvaro in his arms. "No one's ever taken care of me the way you do." He pulled back to look into Alvaro's eyes. "Okay, we'll wait to have full-on sex," he said as he reached down to stroke Alvaro's cock. "Are you sure you cleared this with Godzilla? He seems to have no problem with doing it right here and now."

"And you'd take the advice of a mutated lizard?" Alvaro covered Cande's mouth with his in a long, sweet kiss. Cande continued to shuttle his hand up and down Alvaro's shaft, slicking the suede-skinned rod with the fluid that leaked from the tip.

"Just the head?" Cande wheedled. "You're making enough pre-cum to lubricate King Kong. Come on. Please. I just want to feel a little bit of you inside me."

"I could use my fingers."

Cande sighed. "It's not the same." He spread his legs wider apart. "Come on. Just the tip."

"You really are killing me." Alvaro moaned as Cande ran his thumb over the weeping slit of his dick. "Do what you want."

Cande grinned and eased to the very edge of the desk. Taking a firm grip on Alvaro's shaft, Cande rubbed the head across his entrance. He licked his lips and lowered himself a few millimeters until the tip was resting snugly against his opening. "Oh man," he said breathlessly. "I can't tell you how good that feels."

"I think I might have an idea," Alvaro panted.

"Just a little more pressure." Cande licked his lips again. "Just a little more."

The head of Alvaro's cock popped through the tight ring, and Cande bore down on it. "Damn it!" Alvaro choked out. "I just came."

"Really?"

Alvaro gasped as Cande tightened up again. "Don't!" he yelped as he pulled his hips back.

Cande pouted as Alvaro withdrew. "I wish we could do it again right now," he said.

"You're too much," Alvaro said, gathering his lover into his arms to hug him tightly. "Would you like to, you know…?" Alvaro's voice trailed off.

"Put my dick in you?" Cande finished. He laughed at the look on Alvaro's face. "You can't even say it."

"I'd let you, though, if you wanted to."

"I wouldn't want to if I thought you wouldn't enjoy it. Let's talk about it another time. Right now, you have unfinished business." He looked down.

Alvaro smiled at the sight of Cande's revived erection. "You came too quickly last time," he said. "Let's see if you can do better."

Cande tried, but in a few minutes, he was coming again, panting Alvaro's name as he spurted down Alvaro's throat. He was glad of the help when Alvaro gave him a hand getting his clothes back on and wasn't too proud to lean against his tall boyfriend as they walked home. They were loose-limbed and giddy and anyone who saw them at two a.m. might have concluded that they were drunk. And drunk they were, but not on any liquor ever distilled. They were high on good sex, love and their hopes for the future. Tonight was a dream come true and tomorrow promised to be even better.

"WAKE up!"

Alvaro jumped at the sound of his mother's voice outside his bedroom door. "What is it, Mama?"

"Your breakfast is ready. Come and eat, you and Candelario."

"Okay. Give us a minute."

"It's almost eleven o'clock."

"Damn!" Alvaro shook Cande's shoulder. Cande batted at Alvaro's hand and pulled the blanket over his head. "It's late," Alvaro said. "Come on and wake up."

Cande made a grumpy noise. "It's Sunday."

"I know, but we have a party to go to, remember?"

"All right," Cande whined as he rolled over. "I'm getting up."

"Mama's making breakfast. I'm going to take a quick shower. I'll let you know as soon as I'm done in case you want one."

"Are you kidding? I'm basted in your love juice. Of course I need a shower. I don't suppose we can take one together?"

"Um, I'd feel kind of funny with Mama knowing we were in there together. I'm pretty sure she knows that we're doing stuff, but still...."

"I understand. Go shower and make it quick."

"Okay." Alvaro turned at the door. "Some of that love juice is yours, you know." He dodged the pair of balled-up briefs Cande threw at him. Cande pulled on a pair of pants and a T-shirt and went into the kitchen while Alvaro headed for the bathroom.

"Good morning, honeybee," Mrs. Torres welcomed Cande with a smile and kiss on the cheek.

"Marisol?" Cande said as he took out plates and eating utensils. "I don't mind, but I was wondering why you call me that."

"Because you're so sweet and you work so hard. I thought it was obvious. Maybe you'd rather I didn't call you that when your friends are around?"

"No, it's okay. I've been called a lot worse, believe me."

"I do believe you." Mrs. Torres turned from the stove to look at Cande. "And I'm sorry for all the times you were made to feel different or like you weren't as good as other people."

"It's okay, really. It doesn't bother me anymore."

"Cande," she said, letting the uncomfortable subject drop. "While Alvaro's in the bathroom, I'd like to ask you something." Cande put his head down and pretended to be engrossed in folding napkins. Mrs. Torres smiled at the back of the young man's head. "I don't mean to embarrass you, but how serious is it between you and my son?"

"I love him," Cande said in voice barely above a whisper. "And he says he loves me. I believe him."

"That's a relief. I won't make you talk about it anymore, but I'm glad you have feelings for each other. Alvaro's been so lonely."

"Lonely? Alvaro has more friends than anyone I know."

"He needs someone that he can devote his life to. I'd like it if that someone was you."

"Even though I'm a guy?"

"I don't think I have the right to tell my son who he can love. All I can do is hope that he's happy and that he'll let me have a place in his life after he's grown up."

"Thanks for not being freaked out about it."

"I've been an absentee parent for so long. Poor Alvaro had to raise himself. I just hope he still loves me now that I've returned to the land of the living."

"What are you talking about?" Alvaro said as he came in shirtless with a towel around his neck.

"You, of course," Cande said. "It's all about you."

"I'm glad you finally realized that." Alvaro took off his towel and flicked it at Cande's butt.

"No playing in the kitchen," Mrs. Torres said. "Here, take a plate and find a place to sit. And put on a shirt, son."

"I guess the most chairs are in the front room," Alvaro said, taking a plate.

"Well, go on. You too, Cande. I'll be right there."

They were finishing their breakfast when the phone rang. Alvaro glanced at his mother and then picked up the receiver. He held it away from ear and shouted, "Slow down, Elly." Putting the phone back to his ear, he listened. "Okay," he said. "We'll be there. No, I'm not mad. It's a little weird, but it beats walking. Bye." Alvaro hung up before Eligio could start talking again. "Mr. Cruz will be here to pick us up in an hour."

"Mr. Cruz?" Cande echoed.

"Yeah. Can you believe it? I guess he really doesn't hate kids anymore."

"Hate kids!" Mrs. Torres got up and collected the dishes. "How could anyone hate kids?"

Cande took the plates from her hand. "He's a teacher," he said as he went to the kitchen. In a couple of seconds, Alvaro and his mother heard the water come on. Mrs. Torres looked to Alvaro.

"I have Mr. Cruz for Social Studies just before lunch," Alvaro said. "Up until a few days ago, he was a big pain in the… rear. He treated all his students like we were psycho killers or something."

"That's not right. Teachers are supposed to help the children in their care."

Alvaro grimaced. "I'm not a child, Mama. And I think my school is a little different from the one you went to."

"I'm sorry, son," she said, touching his cheek. "I really let you down. I don't know anything about your school or where you spend your time when you aren't here. But I'm getting better, and things are going to change. It breaks my heart that I missed so many years of your life, and I'm not going to miss anything else if I can help it." She paused. "I don't mean that I'm going to be a pest. I know a young man your age needs some privacy, especially if he's in love. I hope I'm not embarrassing you."

"Um, well, this isn't the sort of conversation I imagined having with you, but I'm glad we can talk this way." Alvaro looked toward the kitchen. "I'm really glad you aren't upset about me and Cande. I know it must be a shock to find out your son is gay."

"It's not what I expected or hoped for," she admitted. "But I can see that you're happy. All any mother really wants is to see her child happy."

"I'm happy," Alvaro assured her.

"Thank you." Mrs. Torres's voice choked off, and it was a few seconds before she could speak again. "Thank you for taking care of me when I should have been taking care of you."

Alvaro took his mother in his arms and held her to his chest. Her tears soaked into the soft cotton of his T-shirt as she hugged him back. "It's okay. Everything's okay now," Alvaro said, kissing her forehead. "I've got my Mama back and that's all that matters."

"You got more than that, I'd say." She lifted her face, smiling through her tears. "What about Cande? And taking second place at the festival?"

"It's kind of like life is giving me all my good luck at once."

"It's about time, don't you think? Now, don't you need to change for Eligio's party?"

"I'm not sure I have anything clean."

"You didn't even notice that I did the laundry yesterday."

"You did the what?" Alvaro stared at her. "That means you went out of the house."

"Only two doors over. Mrs. Lee was very helpful."

"You're out of control," Alvaro said admiringly. "Pretty soon I'll need a GPS to keep up with you."

"Don't be ridiculous. Go. Change your clothes."

Cande came out of the kitchen wiping his hands on a tea towel when Alvaro entered the hall. Their eyes met, and they smiled for no reason at all. Alvaro headed toward the bedroom, and Cande snapped his butt with the damp towel. "Ow!" Alvaro jumped and ran for the door. "What the hell?"

"I'm all about payback," Cande said, rolling the towel again.

Alvaro dashed into his bedroom and shut the door. "I'm sorry I snapped at you with my towel," he said through the wooden panel. "Truce?"

"Truce," Cande said.

Alvaro let Cande in and went to his shallow closet to find a shirt. Cande sorted through the small pile of clothes he'd dumped on the end of the bed. After a few minutes, Alvaro turned from the closet in frustration. "I can't find anything that looks right. Eligio's parents are kind of... you know...."

"Square?"

"Yeah. I keep feeling like I should put on a tie."

"Here," Cande said, holding up a length of black ribbon. "Put on your uniform shirt. If you roll up the sleeves it'll look casual enough, and you can use this."

"For what? My hair's not long enough for—"

"It's a tie," Cande said heavily. "I'll fix it for you; just put on the shirt."

"Man, it's like I went from having no mother to having two," Alvaro complained happily as he slipped on a clean white shirt.

"Oink oink," Cande said absently as he held up a webby black knitted shirt that looked like it would cling like a second skin. "Well, I sure can't wear this, and it's my dressiest shirt."

"Where would you wear something like this?" Alvaro hooked the featherweight shirt on one finger and held it up. "You can see through it in places."

"I wear it when I go to clubs." Cande snatched the shirt back and folded it. "I guess I'll be wearing my button-down too." He took his uniform shirt off the hanger and put it on. Cande left his top two buttons open and did something with his collar that made the plain shirt look like high fashion.

"You make that look good," Alvaro said, watching Cande roll up his sleeves.

"Come here and let me make you gorgeous too." Cande slipped the black ribbon around Alvaro's collar and tied it in a rakish bow. "Not everyone could carry this off," he said. "But it looks great on you." He glanced up at Alvaro's hair. "Can I just…?" He raked his fingers through Alvaro's thick, springy hair, pulling it up and back, curling the longer tendrils behind his lover's ears. "There," he said as he stood back to admire the results.

"Well?" Alvaro spread his arms, pivoting slowly on his heel.

"You're so good-looking," Cande sighed. "That's what I thought the first time I saw you. Only it was more like, *damn, he's hot*. You're ridiculously handsome and you've got that amazing body." He ran his gaze from Alvaro's head to his feet and back. "I'm just so glad that you turned out to be as good as you look."

Alvaro took Cande's chin on his palm and kissed him gently. "I'm glad you gave me a chance to prove you could trust me."

"I still can't believe you didn't walk away from me when you found out about my past."

"You're not the curse you think you are." Alvaro smiled. "You know what? I'm beginning to believe that good things will happen to you if you just let them."

"That's... very optimistic."

"Optimistic, huh? What were you going to say before you changed your mind?"

"Never mind. That would be the old negative me talking. What have I got to complain about?"

"Alvaro. Cande," Mrs. Torres called. "Mr. Cruz is here."

"We'd better get out there and save Mama," Alvaro said.

Cande followed Alvaro to the front room. Mr. Cruz was sitting on the small sofa, and he rose as the young men entered. "Mrs. Torres offered me tea," the teacher said quickly. "I told her not to bother."

"Mama," Alvaro called out. "Mr. Cruz doesn't have time for tea."

Alvaro's mother appeared in the doorway. "No? Are you sure, Mr. Cruz? It will only take a minute."

"No, thank you. We really should be going."

Alvaro went to the door and held it open for the teacher. Mr. Cruz turned and gestured for Alvaro's mother to go first. "Oh, I'm not going," she said. "I... have other plans today."

"What a pity. I was looking forward to a chat with Alvaro's parent. Maybe another time?"

"You'll have to stop by for tea one afternoon."

"I'd like that very much," Mr. Cruz said with a bow. "Good afternoon, Mrs. Torres."

Alvaro glanced at Cande as Mr. Cruz preceded them out the door. Cande shrugged, and Alvaro looked at his mother over Cande's shoulder. Marisol smiled serenely at her son and shooed him out of the apartment. "I don't think I like this," Alvaro muttered to Cande.

"Too bad," Cande said. "She's being really understanding about us. You'll look like a total jerk if you object to her being interested in Mr. Cruz."

"Don't say it out loud!"

"Is everything all right?" Mr. Cruz asked as they reached the bottom of the stairs.

"Yes, sir," the two young men said in unison.

"Thanks for picking us up," Alvaro said as he got into the front passenger seat.

"To be honest, I had nothing else to do today. I'm glad to be spending it with someone besides the people on television."

Alvaro had no reply to this. "Do you know the way to Eligio's house?" he asked.

"I have directions, but feel free to speak up if I make a wrong turn."

"Yes, sir."

Eligio's parents warmly greeted the new arrivals at the door of their modest house and showed them to the back yard. Streamers decorated the trees, and two picnic tables were loaded with food. Eligio's two youngest sisters chased a litter of puppies through the legs of the small crowd. Besides Eligio's family, Kiki, and Leo, there were also several teachers, as well as Mr. Fielder and Mr. Beckermann.

"Check out the cake," Eligio called, and Alvaro and Cande went to join him at the table. Eligio's sisters had obviously helped decorate the huge cake. Across the snowy frosting were written the names of the members of Party of Five in a rainbow of colors with varying degrees of skill.

A surer hand had added yesterday's date beneath the names along with some script.

It was here that the super-group Party of Five got their start.
Best wishes to them as they travel the world bringing
their talent to many lucky people. We know they
won't forget us when they're famous.
Signed, the Friends and Families of Po5.

"I know it's lame," Eligio said apologetically.

Alvaro squeezed the younger boy's shoulder. "No it isn't." He took Cande's hand and waved Kiki and Leo over. The members of Party of Five joined hands for a few moments and then looked up, meeting one another's eyes in turn. Each face wore an identical smile.

They were on their way, and they were going on the journey together.

Epilogue

DANILO ORIENTE straightened his tie and came to attention at his post as he noticed the lady walking toward him. And a lady she was, in contrast to the rest of the audience, which was composed mainly of hyper-frenetic teenage girls. Danilo had worked this grand old theater for thirty-two years from usher to manager, and he'd never seen a crowd like this. Of course, this was the first time that an act like Party of Five had played here. This elegant venue was much too small for the numbers usually drawn by the platinum-selling group, but the story was that the area held sentimental meaning for the five young men who would perform here tonight. Last night, Party of Five had played a sold-out concert to nearly a hundred thousand fans at the L.A. Memorial Coliseum, but this evening would be a little more intimate, to say the least. This Deco era auditorium barely seated five thousand, and the proceeds of each ticket sale had been donated to a children's cancer fund. The popular band was clearly not here to make money; after two years at the top of the charts, they had plenty of wealth and the fame that goes along with it. It was hard for Danilo to believe that the members of Party of Five were once a gang of *delincuentes* attending the Catholic boys' school a few blocks away. It was entirely possible that he had chased them away from spray-painting their names on the theater's back wall sometime in the past. And not that long ago, since the oldest of the group was twenty-three.

Danilo shook his head at the thought of being so young and so successful, wondering what it felt like to be lifted so quickly from the streets to the stars. When the young men had arrived a few hours earlier, he'd seen no signs that they had let it go to their heads. They hadn't swaggered in dripping gold and diamonds surrounded by an entourage of hangers-on. They had shown up ready for business, running through a rehearsal and sound check in well-worn workout clothes before getting into their costumes and makeup. Danilo couldn't honestly say he was a fan of their R & B flavored pop—he was partial to traditional *Son cubano* music—but he approved of their professionalism and their manners. Courtesy was important to Danilo.

He bowed slightly as the lady stopped in front of the door he manned. He didn't stare, of course, but brief glances assured him that his first impression of her was correct. From her simply but elegantly dressed hair to her low-heeled silver pumps, she was the definition of gracious dignity and style. He couldn't have named the designer of her white satin sheath or the style of her short beaded jacket, but he knew that they suited her svelte figure in a way that managed to be both modest and alluring. The term *age appropriate* meant something to Danilo; he supposed he was old-fashioned, but he had strong opinions on propriety. It was one of the things that made him so good at his job. It had been some time since he had done an usher's duty, but tonight the right hand balcony was reserved for VIPs, and he thought it fitting that a senior representative of the theater be on hand to greet them. Most of the guests of Party of Five were already seated, but the velvet-roped front row was still empty. Danilo would bet that one of those seats belonged to this woman.

"Good evening, ma'am," he said.

"It's a very good evening," she answered, her eyes sparkling with excitement.

"May I help you find your seat?"

"Someone's joining me. I'd like to wait if that's all right."

"Of course, ma'am. I'm assuming you're one of the guests of honor."

"That's what they tell me." She smiled warmly. "I'm Alvaro Torres's mother."

"There you are!"

Danilo and Marisol turned toward the speaker and saw a slight man in glasses hurrying toward them. "Brooks," Alvaro's mother said delightedly. "How wonderful to see you again!"

Brooks Matheson stopped beside Marisol and made a little bow. "It's great to see you again too."

Marisol kissed his cheek and drew back. "You look like your new job agrees with you."

"I'm still working with talented young people so I haven't really given anything up, and Po5's corporation pays a lot better than the school system."

"I'm sure you're missed at the school."

"We can chat later. Alvaro's been pacing for the last twenty minutes worrying about you."

"Traffic was difficult. I've forgotten what it's like to try and drive into this neighborhood after five o'clock."

"How is the townhouse working out? But what am I saying? That's the first thing Alvaro is going to ask you. I've never seen anyone prouder of a purchase."

"I love the house, and I'll love it even more when my son comes to visit me in it."

Mr. Matheson glanced at his watch. "I have orders to take you down to the dressing room to say hello. I think we just have enough time."

"Don't worry that this door will be closed," Danilo spoke up. "I'll wait right here for the lady."

"Shall we go?" Mr. Matheson offered his arm.

"I hate to go without Martin." Alvaro's mother cast a glance at the stairs. As if she'd summoned him, a man appeared and came toward them.

"Sorry I kept you waiting," he said. "I had a heck of a time getting through the crowd in the lobby." He put a finger in his ear and wiggled it. "I may be partially deaf from the screaming."

"You wouldn't be happy without something to complain about, Cruz," Mr. Matheson said.

Martin Cruz smiled. "My students give me enough grief without me inventing new trouble."

"Ready to go backstage?"

"Mrs. Cruz, are you ready?"

Marisol smiled at her husband of two years. "Yes, I am, Mr. Cruz."

"WHERE is she?" Alvaro said for perhaps the thousandth time.

Cande sat down on Alvaro's thighs, facing him. With deft gestures, he untangled the gold chains around his lover's neck, letting his hands run down the bare chest, stroking lightly. "She'll be here."

Alvaro looked toward the door of the empty dressing room. "We should get out there," he said.

Cande shook his head, silky red-amber hair swinging against his cheeks. "You need to stay right here and keep your head on straight. If you go out there, you'll find a dozen things wrong and blow your stack." He reached up to smooth Alvaro's eyebrows with his thumbs in soothing repetitive motions. "Nothing bad has happened. You know Mr. Cruz would never let anything happen to your mama."

"I know you're right, but I still would've liked to see her before the show." Alvaro sighed. "Our first show in the old neighborhood."

"It was a good idea to give a show for our local fan club and invite all our old friends from the nabe. Not that I have many, but it's got to be a kick for you guys to know that your old teachers who said you'd never amount to anything will be in the audience."

Alvaro smiled at last. "Kiki calls it Leo's Revenge, but somehow I don't feel the need to shove anything in anyone's face anymore." He put his arms around Cande's waist and looked into his eyes. "I've got you. What else could I possibly want?"

"You seemed to get pretty excited over the gold and platinum records."

"Yeah, well, a guy needs a reason to celebrate now and then."

"You're all the reason I need." Cande smiled back at his boyfriend. "We've been together for almost five years, and I'm still thankful every day that you took a chance on me."

"I just wanted to get into your jeans."

"Asshole." Cande smacked the back of Alvaro's head. "You're lucky I know you're kidding."

"I'm lucky in general since I met you."

"That was much better. Allow me to say that you're the handsomest, strongest, bravest, most talented man in the world and I love you to pieces."

"If you must." Alvaro grabbed a double handful of Cande's butt and pulled him closer. "Allow me to say that you have one of the premier asses of the century."

"Are you getting turned on?"

"Of course. I'm within ten miles of you, right?"

Cande chuckled. "You're crazy; never change."

"I won't, babe: not my heart or my underwear."

Cande laughed again and leaned down to give Alvaro a kiss. They jumped when the door opened, but stayed where they were. No one that wasn't part of the inner circle would come in without knocking and their closest friends all knew about their relationship. They smiled when they recognized Gisela the continuity girl, also known as Eligio's fiancée.

"Jeez, you two," Gisela said. "Get out of each other's grill for five seconds. Damn, why don't you go ahead and make it legal like the other two?"

"You want to have a double wedding?" Alvaro asked.

She laughed. "Elly would expire on the spot if I suggested it. Turn his big day into a circus? I think not. No, you'll just have to do it on the down-low like Leo and Kiki."

"You're right," Cande sighed. "But someday…."

"Hey," Alvaro said, cupping Cande's cheek on his palm. "If you want to come out tonight, I'll announce it from the stage. I'm not ashamed of you or our love."

"It means the world to me that you feel that way," Cande answered, "but I still think we should wait. Let's build up our power base a little more first."

"You see?" Alvaro looked to Gisela. "It's not me; it's him."

"Yeah, I see," she said. "I also see your mother. You want to say hi before the show starts?"

"Damn it, woman! Why didn't you say so in the first place?" Alvaro got up, Cande sliding off his lap like a cat. Arms around each other's waists, they followed Gisela out the door.

Marisol started crying the second she saw Alvaro. Tears began running down Alvaro's cheeks as he took her in his arms and hugged her tight. It wasn't long before everyone in their vicinity was crying or struggling not to. The new Mrs. Cruz let go of her son with one arm to gather Cande in, kissing him on the cheek as she pulled him closer. In another two minutes, Leo, Kiki, Eligio, and their families joined the group hug. Life for the last few years had been a series of triumphs as Po5 sailed with seeming effortlessness from one pinnacle to the next, but none of the awards, sold-out shows, or accolades from their peers could match this moment. They were home, safe and sound in the arms of their families, their friends, and their lovers.

Alvaro lifted his head as the chanting, clapping and stomping of the crowd crashed into the backstage area. His eyes met Cande's and traveled on to Kiki, Leo, and Eligio. He grinned as he let go of his mother, and the group hug broke up. "I think we're being called out," he said.

Leo's grin matched Alvaro's as he knocked fists with his old friend. "Yeah and what? We know how to bring it."

"I love the way you roll, honey," Kiki told his husband.

"Come on. Stop screwing around, you guys," Eligio said. "We should have been on stage ten minutes ago."

"Lead the way," Alvaro said. "What are you waiting for?"

Eligio didn't wait to be told twice. His long legs flashed in silver-fringed jeans as he bounded across the backstage area. Kiki and Leo followed him, their faces glowing as the noise swelled at their appearance on stage. Alvaro turned at the brink to give Cande a quick kiss as they disentangled their fingers. The excitement and joy that shone in his eyes was mirrored in his lover's gaze. They had gambled on each other, risking it all, never expecting to get something for nothing, and now they had everything.

CONNIE BAILEY is a Luddite who can't live without her computer. She's an acrophobic who loves to fly, a fault-finding pessimist who, nonetheless, is always surprised when something bad happens, and an antisocialite who loves her friends like family. She's held a number of jobs in many disparate arenas to put food on the table, but writing is the occupation that feeds her soul.

Connie lives with her ultralight designer husband at a small grass-strip airfield halfway between Disney World and Busch Gardens. Logic and reality have had little to do with her life, and she likes it that way.

Visit her Web site at http://www.conniebailey.com/ and her blog at http://baileymoyes.livejournal.com/.

Also by CONNIE BAILEY

http://www.dreamspinnerpress.com

Young Love from DREAMSPINNER PRESS

www.ingramcontent.com/pod-product-compliance
Lightning Source LLC
Chambersburg PA
CBHW070006260626
47159CB00005B/1692